LUCY D

Husky

— in a —

Hut

Illustrations by Ann Baum

Hodder
Children's
Books

a division of Hodder Headline Limited

Special thanks to Stephen Cole

**Thanks also to C. J. Hall, B.Vet.Med., M.R.C.V.S., for reviewing
the veterinary information contained in this book.**

Animal Ark is a trademark of Working Partners Limited
Text copyright © 2002 Working Partners Limited
Created by Working Partners Limited, London W6 0QT
Original series created by Ben M. Baglio
Illustrations copyright © 2002 Ann Baum

First published in Great Britain in 2002
by Hodder Children's Books

The right of Lucy Daniels to be identified as the author of this work
has been asserted by her in accordance with the Copyright, Designs
and Patents Act 1988.

For more information about Animal Ark,
please contact www.animalark.co.uk

2 4 6 8 10 9 7 5 3 1

A Catalogue record for this book is available from the British
Library

ISBN 0 340 90304 X

Typeset in Baskerville by Avon DataSet Ltd,
Bidford-on-Avon, Warwickshire

Printed and bound in Great Britain by
Clays Ltd, St Ives plc

The paper and board used in this paperback by
Hodder Children's Books are natural recyclable products
made from wood grown in sustainable forests.
The manufacturing processes conform to the environmental
regulations of the country of origin.

Hodder Children's Books
a division of Hodder Headline Limited
338 Euston Road
London NW1 3BH

One

'Come on!' Mandy Hope called from the finish line, her voice almost lost as the crowd cheered and shouted all around her. 'You can do it!'

The two dog sleds were getting closer, each pulled along the snowy track by a team of straining huskies. Mandy's cheeks were flushed, both with excitement and from the icy wind, and she was grinning from ear to ear. She had seen so much amazing wildlife while visiting Canada with her parents. Seals, polar bears, and now racing huskies – pulling their drivers in wooden sleds across the frozen ground.

Both drivers were concentrating hard, shouting instructions at the dogs in Inuktitut – the native language of Baffin Island.

Emily Hope shielded her eyes from the glare of sunlight on snow as she peered up the track. 'Which sled is Simonie driving?' she asked.

'That one, Mum!' cried Mandy. She pointed to the sled that was just edging into the lead.

'Come on, Simonie!' bellowed Mandy's dad, Adam Hope, who was almost jumping up and down in the snow. 'Not far now!'

Simonie Nanogak owned a company that ran dog-sled tours and the Hopes were staying with him and his family. Mr and Mrs Hope were both vets who ran a busy surgery called Animal Ark in the Yorkshire village of Welford, thousands of miles away from this snowy island. A Canadian university that was researching the effects of tourism and environmental change on sub-Arctic wildlife had funded their expedition. Kimmirut, a little seaside community on Baffin Island, was the last stop on their tour. Simonie's was not the only dog-sled company in the town, and friendly local rivalry made the dog-sled races as tense as they were popular with tourists and locals alike. For one afternoon every week a clutch of back streets in the little town were closed off to traffic and used as a racetrack and echoed again with the centuries-old sound of huskies pulling sleds over the thick snow.

'Watch out, Simonie!' shouted Mr Hope, pointing wildly at the other driver. 'He's catching you up!'

The barks of the dogs grew louder as the sleds bumped and scraped closer to the finish line, skimming faster and faster over the frozen ground. On each side of the track the crowds surged forward, cheering on the two teams. The huskies' eyes were narrowed against the rushing wind, tongues lolling out of their mouths as they panted with exertion. Not far to go now, if Simonie Nanogak could just hold on . . .

'Yes!' Mandy cried, as Simonie's sled flew across the line scored in the slushy snow. 'The winner!' A huge cheer went up from the crowd.

The other driver came in just behind Simonie. His sled skidded to a halt in a flurry of snow. Mandy saw the man thump his fist against his sled in frustration, an angry scowl on his face. Even through the thick padding of his thermal clothes, the man looked thin and pinched, in contrast to Simonie's open, friendly face.

'Come on,' said Emily Hope. 'Let's go and congratulate Simonie.'

'And his dogs, too!' Mandy added.

'Looks like we'll have to get in line,' smiled Mr Hope, pointing out two new arrivals who were pushing through the excited throng of people. 'Pani and Mary have got there ahead of us!'

Mary Nanogak was a kind-looking woman with tanned skin and a shy smile. She was carrying a heavy plastic container full of water to give the dogs. Her daughter, Pani, held a big pile of dog dishes. At eleven years old, Pani was a year younger than Mandy. She had dark brown hair that came down to her waist and deep brown eyes. She and Mandy had become friends from the moment they'd met, just yesterday.

'A bit different from Welford, isn't it?' Mandy said, as she and her parents skirted round the crowds to reach the Nanogaks more quickly. The wind had picked up, and Mandy pulled her scarf around her face to keep out the biting needles of icy air.

Adam Hope nodded. 'I'll be glad to get

back to a good Yorkshire winter to warm up a bit!' he joked.

Mary Nanogak saw them coming and smiled. She nudged her husband, and he looked up and waved.

'Congratulations, Simonie!' grinned Emily Hope.

'Yes, that was a brilliant race!' Mandy said, tugging down her fleecy hood and shaking out her blonde hair. 'Well done!'

Simonie shook his head modestly. 'It is all the dogs,' he said with a smile.

'You have them superbly trained,' Adam Hope observed.

'We start when they're puppies,' Simonie explained. 'Mary works with them every day.'

'You must watch us train while you're here,' Mary Nanogak said, as she started to undo the buckles and catches on the leather harnesses that bound all six dogs together.

'We'd love to,' Mandy said. 'Maybe I'll pick up some tips for James to try out on Blackie!' James Hunter was Mandy's best friend back in Welford. She grinned at the thought of his black Labrador pulling a dog sled to victory.

Pani was crouching down in the snow as she laid out the water dishes and fussed the dogs. Mandy squatted down next to her and began to pour the water.

'Another race won,' Pani said proudly. She patted Nanook, the lead husky. 'She runs like the wind!'

'She certainly does,' Mandy replied, as the husky nuzzled against her. Nanook was a special sort of husky called a Canadian Inuit dog. Like the others, she had a short snout, pale blue eyes and long slender legs. One of her short triangular ears pointed straight up while the other curled over, and this, together with her snowy white coat, marked her out from the other dogs.

'You're really lucky, having so many dogs to look after,' said Mandy.

'I know,' Pani said as she stroked Nanook's back. 'I love them all, but Nanook is extra special. We were both born on the same day, so we're almost twins.'

'That's lovely,' said Mandy. Then she frowned as she noticed that Nanook was limping slightly as she moved away. 'Hey girl, come here!' Mandy called. 'What's wrong?'

Nanook looked back and cocked her head to one side. Mandy reached forward and gently lifted one paw. She soon spotted the problem.

'Is she OK?' Pani asked worriedly.

'Fine,' Mandy reassured her. 'She's just got a snowy pebble caught in the pads of her foot.' She gently prodded the snowy lump free. Nanook put her paw uncertainly back on the ground. Then she reached up and licked Mandy on the cheek.

'You're very privileged!' Pani said

admiringly. 'Nanook hardly ever kisses anyone. You'll be her friend for life now!'

'It doesn't take Mandy long to make friends with *any* animal!' Emily Hope laughed. 'Well done for getting rid of that stone, love. These huskies have tough pads, but they still need to be checked regularly.'

All around them, the dogs thirstily lapped up their water. They looked up now and then with keen eyes to take in the busy scene. After drinking half her water, Nanook gave herself a shake and wandered away.

'If I'd run as fast as they just have, I think I'd want to drink a bit more than that,' Mandy observed, looking at the half-full water dish.

'It's important they don't get dehydrated, but they're too hot to think of drinking gallons right now,' Mary explained. 'That pint or so will help them start to cool down. They'll want to drink more when we get back home.'

'We'll be heading back soon,' Pani added. 'The dogs need feeding and clearing out.' She paused shyly. 'Perhaps we can do it together?'

Mandy grinned. 'I'd love to!' The dogs had already been settled in for the night by the time the Hopes had arrived yesterday, and Mandy was dying to help out in the busy kennels.

As she spoke, one of the bigger dogs started to nuzzle Okpik, a small dark husky who had brought up the rear in the sled team.

'Careful, Sedna,' Pani said firmly. Then she turned to Mandy. 'She's only playing but sometimes she can be rough.'

Sedna batted at Okpik with a big paw, so Mandy gently pushed the two of them apart. Okpik circled round her and lay on his back in the snow, and Mandy rubbed his tummy. His fur was velvety soft, and so thick that his skin was warm and dry in spite of the snow.

'Another friend for life!' grinned Pani.

Adam Hope chuckled, and stooped to help Mary gather up the harnesses. 'Here, let me give you a hand.'

'There's no need, really,' Mary replied in her slightly accented English.

'Are you sure?' Mr Hope persisted.

'I know what you're up to, Adam,' Simonie said with a grin. 'You're only offering because you want my wife to make more of that char stew you ate last night!'

'The thought hadn't crossed my mind!' Adam Hope said innocently, stroking his bearded chin. 'Well, if you're sure I can't help out here, Simonie,' he went on, 'I think I'll just pop over and offer my sympathies to the losing team.'

Simonie briefly looked over at the skinny man he had beaten in the race, and his face hardened. 'If you feel you should,' he said stiffly.

'More dogs to fuss over!' Mandy said,

beaming at Pani, but the girl just looked away awkwardly.

'You two go on. I'll wait for you here,' said Mrs Hope.

'OK.' Mandy nodded. The happy mood seemed to have faded suddenly. Was it something she'd said?

'Perhaps this race wasn't as friendly as we thought it was,' remarked Mandy's dad as the two of them strode off through the snow.

Mandy nodded towards Simonie's rival in the race. 'He looked really angry when he lost.'

'Doesn't look much happier now, does he?' Mr Hope observed. 'Perhaps he had a bet on his own dogs winning!'

As they drew closer, a burly man in a green overcoat walked over to join the sled driver. 'Was that really the best your dogs could do, Mr Tupilak?' the newcomer asked in a Canadian accent. 'You told me your dogs were the finest on Baffin Island. Maybe I should go on Simonie Nanogak's sled-trip after all.'

Mr Tupilak smiled coldly. 'At the prices *he* charges?' He shook his head and put an arm round the man, leading him away. 'Come, Mr Ellison. We'll reach an agreement, OK?'

'When's Simonie's next sled-trip, Dad?' Mandy asked, feeling suddenly excited.

Adam Hope smiled at her. 'I think he has a few each week. We'll have to ask him.' Then he turned back to the two men and frowned slightly. 'It looks like Mr Tupilak is Simonie's competition in more ways than one, if he runs a dog-sled company too.'

But Mandy's attention had been taken by Mr Tupilak's huskies. There were no bowls of water laid out for these dogs, no fussing and petting from their owner. Instead, they were biting at the snow to cool themselves down.

Mandy went over to see them. She

crouched down and stroked one of the
dogs, but it shrank away from her touch.
Its leg was caught up in the harness, and
automatically she started to untangle it. The
dog whimpered.

'Wait a minute,' Adam Hope muttered. He
crouched down next to the dog and started
to examine its front leg.

'What is it, Dad?' Mandy asked, concerned.

'His dew-claw, I think,' said Mr Hope.
'Look there, he's—'

'What are you doing, please?' came a low,
quiet voice behind them. Mandy jumped. It
was Mr Tupilak. He had finished his
discussion with Mr Ellison and was standing
over them, his eyes dark as coals.

Adam Hope didn't look up, but carried
on examining the husky and the harness.
'These are your dogs, I take it?'

'They are my *business*,' the man said, 'and
I would prefer *you* to mind *yours*.'

Mandy looked up, shocked by his

rudeness. Before she could stop herself she blurted out, 'But your dog is hurt!'

The man gave her a mocking smile. 'You watch one race, you become the experts, yes?'

'My daughter's quite right,' Mr Hope said firmly, getting back up. 'I'm a vet, although you don't need to be an expert to see that this dog has caught his dew-claw on the harness here.'

'Dew-claw?' Mr Tupilak frowned.

Adam deftly unclipped the leather reins and let the strap go slack so the dog could lower its leg. He pointed to the little claw curving from the dog's foreleg. 'Here,' he said patiently. 'It's a kind of half-formed extra toe – many dogs have them.'

'Oh,' said Mr Tupilak. 'That.' The husky padded off a little stiffly, but stopped dead when his owner snapped a command. Mr Tupilak crouched down and glanced at the husky's leg. 'A scratch, that is all.'

'It's simple enough to remove the dew-claws of working dogs when they're puppies,' Mr Hope said coolly. 'It avoids possible injuries later in life. Your dog was lucky this time; he'll be fine, but a torn claw could stop him racing for—'

'I've heard enough of this nonsense,' Mr Tupliak interrupted, glowering at them both. 'I don't need a vet, I can look after my own dogs. Now if you will excuse me? I have things to do.'

Mandy watched helplessly as the man turned on his heel and left. 'How can he be so uncaring?'

Mr Hope sighed. 'Come on, Mandy. There's nothing more we can do here.'

They trudged back to Emily Hope and the others. Simonie Nanogak was watching them, his broad face still grim.

'Who *is* that man?' Mandy asked him.

'Thomas Tupilak,' said Simonie. 'He's bad news. Runs a sled-tour agency like Mary and me, but . . .' He sighed. 'I just can't match his prices.'

'Yes, he was bragging about his rates to a potential customer,' Mr Hope said thoughtfully. 'How can he charge so little?'

'He employs fewer staff in his kennels, for one thing,' Simonie said. 'And he looks after his animals himself to save on vet bills.'

Adam Hope shook his head. 'Then it's the dogs who'll pay in the end.'

'Exactly,' Simonie nodded.

Mandy's heart went out to Thomas Tupilak's huskies as they trotted off after their master into a waiting trailer. 'Can't he be reported?' she asked.

'We've tried,' Mary Nanogak said. 'But there's never enough evidence.'

'He's . . . what would you call him? A slippery customer.' Simonie shook his head. 'I auctioned some of Nanook's pups a year or so ago. He knew I'd never have let them go to his business willingly, so he paid someone to bid for him.'

'Like you say, a slippery customer,' Mr Hope agreed.

'We have another word for Tupilak here in Kimmirut,' Pani said. '*Tiriaq.*'

Mandy frowned. 'Tiriaq?'

'It is an Inuit word,' Simonie explained. 'It means "weasel".'

Mandy nodded. The name fitted Tupilak perfectly.

'Well, Simonie,' Adam Hope said, trying to brighten the mood, 'just watching the race has given me an appetite. When you mentioned char stew earlier . . .'

Pani smiled. 'Yes, Dad, you won the race, we should have a special dinner!'

'I'll peel a few spuds if you like,' Mr Hope offered brightly.

'Spuds?' Mary Nanogak looked puzzled.

'He means we'll be glad to help out with supper,' Emily Hope said.

'And *I'll* be glad to help out in the dog yard!' Mandy declared.

'So what are we waiting for?' asked Pani with a grin. 'Let's go!'

Two

'Nearly home,' Simonie said, as he steered the truck off the main street and down the long frozen driveway to his house.

It was just mid-afternoon but already the sky was darkening. Mandy listened to the snuffles and excited whines of the huskies in the back of the truck. She smiled. They knew they were almost home too.

The truck journey back to the Nanogaks' house had lasted just twenty minutes, but that was time enough for a fresh blizzard to blow up. The rows of dark town houses, now dusted with white, gave way to emptier streets. Only a few houses and bungalows dotted the roadside.

Mandy jumped as she saw a shadowy figure standing in the middle of the track leading to the Nanogaks' house.

'Don't worry, Mandy,' said Pani. 'It's just Grandad. He lives in the next street. He's meant to be retired but he always comes round to help out!'

The figure turned and raised a hand in welcome, and Mandy saw he was holding a broom, clearing the path of snow. She waved back.

Simonie slowed the truck and gave the man a thumbs-up through the window. 'Thanks, Dad!' The dogs all joined in, a chorus of whines and distinctive husky yowls as the truck rumbled past. Mandy saw the old man's weathered face crease into a broad grin.

Simonie parked the truck and Adam and Emily Hope clambered out first, their boots sinking into the crisp snow.

'I don't think I'll ever be warm again!' Mrs Hope exclaimed, sneezing noisily.

'Sounds like you're getting a cold,' said Mr Hope.

'A bit of exercise with this lot will soon warm you up,' Simonie said, opening the back of the truck and letting the dogs out.

'I'm feeling so cold, I think I'll wait for you inside,' Emily Hope said.

'Do you want to go inside to warm up with your mother, Mandy?' asked Mary Nanogak.

'No thanks,' said Mandy, happily accepting two of the dog leads from Simonie and letting Okpik and Nanook lead her to a large, fenced-in yard. She looked around, narrowing her eyes against the bright floodlights, which kept out the gathering dusk. The freshly swept dog yard was bordered by pens of differing sizes around a

large exercise area. Each dog had its own
kennel raised above the snow to stop the
floor getting damp, and with a hinged roof
that lifted up so that the bedding inside
could be changed easily. There was a small,
enclosed run attached to each kennel.
Beyond the high chain-link fence there was
another, smaller yard.

'What's through there?' Mandy asked, as
she unclipped the leads from Okpik and
Nanook.

'Heat pen,' Simonie said. 'We keep any
females on heat in there to avoid unwanted
litters.'

Adam Hope nodded towards a wooden
building at the far end of the yard. 'And
that's the whelping house?'

Pani nodded happily. 'To look after the
puppies.'

Suddenly, Okpik started barking, bringing
the other dogs in the yard out to greet the
arrivals. They each came out from their

kennels and started barking back. Soon the air was filled with the unusual 'woo-woo!' sounds, quite different from the 'woof' which Mandy was more used to.

'I think they're after room service,' Adam Hope joked, covering his ears.

'And here it comes now,' Mandy said, spotting Mary Nanogak coming out from the house, pulling a large barrel behind her on a creaking wooden cart. As Simonie let the other dogs out of their pens into the exercise yard, Pani went over and helped her mum pour liquid into a large trough by the yard entrance.

Mandy caught a strong whiff of fish, and wrinkled up her nose. 'It smells like the water's gone off!' she said.

Simonie smiled. 'The water is cold. The huskies need some encouragement to drink it down in this freezing weather, so we add some fish stock.' He pointed to the dogs jostling each other as they lapped eagerly from the trough. 'As you can see, it smells good to them!'

Just then, Pani's grandad walked back into the yard. Nanook, who hadn't joined the other dogs at the trough, rushed over to greet him. The old man crouched down stiffly and started to run his hands over the husky in a very deliberate way.

'It's like he's examining her, Dad,' Mandy said, surprised and a bit concerned. She walked over to join the old man and Nanook. 'Is she all right?' she asked.

The old man looked up at her and smiled kindly. 'Oh yes.' His English was as slow and deliberate as his hands on Nanook's back. He called over to Simonie. 'A little more fresh meat in Nanook's feed tonight, I think. She needs more fat in her diet, and we must keep her water levels up.'

'You can tell that just from feeling her?' Mandy asked, amazed.

The man nodded. Then he held out his

hand. 'My name is Solomon. How do you do?'

'Pleased to meet you.' Mandy smiled and shook his hand. 'I'm Mandy Hope.'

Solomon smiled back. 'Come, Mandy.' He pressed her gloved hand against Nanook's warm flank. 'You try. Feel the ribs, the spine, the hip bones.'

Mandy tried to copy Solomon's careful movements and he nodded approvingly.

Simonie watched them. 'After forty years there's not much my father doesn't know about huskies,' he said. 'A well-conditioned sled dog needs very careful feeding. When it's really cold, the dogs need more just to keep their body temperature normal.'

'It sounds like mealtimes are really complicated,' Mandy remarked, straightening up.

'They can be,' Simonie agreed. 'Well, I've got some errands to run in town,' he said. 'I'll see you all later.'

Mandy and the others waved goodbye as he jumped back into the truck and drove out of the yard. Nanook watched him go, then trotted off in the other direction. Rather than play with the other dogs, the snow-white husky crossed the yard and stood alone by the chain-link fence, looking out into the darkness.

'That's Nanook,' said Solomon, nodding thoughtfully. 'She's not so happy mixing with the other dogs.'

'But she leads the sled team,' said Mandy, frowning.

'Yes – but she will *only* lead,' Solomon said. 'She will not run with the others. Just like a lone wolf.'

'I wonder what she's looking at,' Mandy murmured. There was something rather melancholy about Nanook standing all alone while the other dogs were enjoying themselves, leaping and playing in the snow.

'Who can say?' Solomon answered. Then

he smiled warmly. 'But do not worry. Nanook is happy here, I assure you!'

'Mandy, come and meet Allicee,' called Pani. Allicee gave a high-pitched bark. She was smaller and darker than the other dogs.

'She's lovely,' said Mandy, hurrying over to say hello. 'How old is she?'

'Just six months,' Pani replied.

'Old enough to learn the ropes though?' Adam Hope said to Mary Nanogak, nodding at the leather harness in her hands.

Mary sighed. 'Allicee finds running with the others frightening. She doesn't enjoy it at all.'

Mandy looked sympathetically at the dark little dog. 'So what will you do?'

'She just needs some time to get used to the harness,' Pani said, taking the leather straps from her mother. 'We'll join her to an older dog with this neckline and let them run around for a few minutes.'

Mandy nodded as she helped Pani clip the special lead on to Allicee's collar.

'Saliq can take her,' said Mary Nanogak, pointing to a stocky black and white dog. 'He'll be glad of a run before the sled-trip tomorrow.'

'A sled-trip to where?' asked Mr Hope.

'Into the Katannilik Territorial Park,' Mary told him. 'It's a three-day trip, travelling by sled all the way.'

Mandy gave her dad an excited look. 'It sounds fantastic!'

'Do you have any places left?' asked Mr Hope.

'I'm not sure,' Mary said. 'Simonie's gone to collect the customers' deposits and to check they're all still coming. I'm sorry we didn't mention it last night. We've got you booked in for the short sled-trip to the coast and back on Friday, but we thought you'd be too busy to spare three days on an outing.'

Mr Hope nodded. 'Well, I suppose we do

need to collate figures on local tourism, as well as studying—'

Mandy interrupted him. 'But a sled-trip would be amazing! What a great way to explore Baffin Island!'

Her dad grinned. 'You've got a good point there, Mandy!'

'We'll ask Dad tonight,' Pani promised, jogging over to fetch Saliq. 'It'd be great to have you on the trip!'

'Fingers crossed,' said Mandy.

As Pani fixed the other end of the neckline to Saliq, Allicee began to tremble. 'Oh dear,' Pani said. 'Allicee, you *have* to get used to the harness . . .'

Mandy crouched down and whispered in the husky's ear. 'It's all right, girl. You'll be all right.' Suddenly, she had an idea. She walked away from the dogs, then slapped her palms against her thighs. 'Come on, Allicee,' she called, jogging on the spot. 'Come on, chase after me!'

Allicee watched her for a few moments, then took a few steps forward.

'Good dog!' Mandy called, jogging off in a new direction. Allicee followed, starting to get excited. Saliq followed as the puppy pulled on the neckline. As Mandy started running a little faster round the yard, Saliq got more interested in the game. With his longer legs, he was soon leading Allicee along after him. After a minute or so, red-faced and puffing, Mandy slowed down and leaned against the fence next to her dad. But Saliq wasn't stopping, and neither was Allicee – they were enjoying themselves too much by now! Running around in broad circles, the young dog suddenly looked like she'd been running in harness for years.

'OK, Allicee, that's enough for now,' said Mary Nanogak, clapping her hands. 'Nice work, Mandy,' she added.

'Yes, well done,' said Mr Hope. 'Now, let's

get inside before we catch cold like your poor mother!'

'Oh, all right,' Mandy sighed. 'But can I help again in the morning, Pani?'

'Just try and get out of it!' said Pani with a grin.

Mandy and her dad stamped the snow from their boots in the Nanogaks' porch, and went into the kitchen to take off their heavy coats.

Emily Hope was sitting at the big wooden table with a steaming mug of coffee and a pile of research notes. Her red hair hung limply over her face, and her eyes were red-rimmed and sore-looking.

'How are you feeling, Mum?' Mandy asked her.

'Not wonderful,' she confessed with a sniff. 'But I've checked our e-mails. There's one from James for you.'

'Great!' Mandy cried, running up the stairs to the laptop in her parents' room. James's e-mails kept her up to date on everything that was going on back home.

Soon she was writing James a hasty reply, telling him all about her recent adventures, and how much she hoped she'd be able to go on the trip tomorrow. Then she realised that it was the middle of the night back home. By the time James received the e-mail, she'd already know one way or the other.

A loud sneeze greeted Mandy as she walked back downstairs. 'Bless you, Mum,' said Mandy. 'Has Dad told you about the sled-trip?'

Emily Hope nodded. 'It's a shame, but I don't think I'm feeling up to three days' cross-country in the snow.'

'*If* there's room at all,' Adam Hope reminded them both cautiously.

It felt like hours before Simonie returned from his errands, just in time for dinner. The rest of them were already seated round the Nanogaks' big kitchen table, savouring the smells from Mary's stove. Mandy had been bursting to ask Simonie about the trip the second he came through the door, but something about the gloomy look on his broad face made her hesitate.

Mary served up fish stew and *poutine*, a delicious French-Canadian dish of chips covered in melted cheese. But while Mandy and her family tucked in along with Pani and Solomon, Simonie took his place at the table in a grim silence.

'Everything all right, Simonie?' asked Mary Nanogak.

Simonie shook his head. 'Five people have dropped out of tomorrow's trip.'

'Five!' Pani exclaimed.

'Out of the ten we had signed up to go.' Simonie sighed wearily. 'They say they're travelling with Thomas Tupilak instead, later in the week.'

'How many can you fit on a sled, Simonie?' asked Adam Hope.

'About six,' he replied. 'Two sleds can comfortably hold ten tourists, plus a driver for each.'

Mandy felt her heart sinking. 'So you've got just enough people to fill one sled tomorrow,' she said in a small voice.

'And that will barely cover the cost of the expedition,' Solomon pointed out. 'You need two sleds to be profitable.'

'But . . . Dad and I would love to come,' said Mandy. 'Couldn't *we* go in the second sled?'

Simonie shook his head sadly. 'I'm sorry, Mandy. It must be a full sled before I can afford to hire another driver, and to feed and water another team of dogs.'

Mandy nodded and glumly carried on with her dinner. She tried not to be too disappointed. Maybe she was missing out on an amazing Arctic expedition, but Simonie was losing a part of his livelihood. And if Thomas Tupilak kept his prices low, perhaps Simonie and Mary would be put out of business altogether.

Adam Hope took a mouthful of stew. 'Well, Simonie, if anyone else drops out, we'll happily take their places.'

'There's always the half-day sled-trip to the coast on Friday,' Emily Hope reminded Mandy. 'I know it's not quite the same, but it's something.'

Mandy nodded and forced a smile. But as she got into bed that night, Mandy hoped desperately that somehow she could go on the three-day trip into the park. She lay in the darkness for ages, mentally counting endless herds of caribou, and still sleep wouldn't come. The morning seemed as far away as Animal Ark was, on the other side of the world.

Three

A loud ringing woke Mandy from her fitful sleep. She reached automatically for her alarm clock – then remembered she hadn't set it. The noise was the Nanogaks' telephone ringing in the hall.

Mandy staggered out of bed, dressed quickly, and headed for the bathroom.

'You're up early, Mandy!' Adam Hope remarked as he came out ahead of her. His brown hair was wet and ruffled and a towel hung round his neck.

'Is there any news about the sled-trip?' Mandy asked.

Mr Hope grinned. 'Let's go and see, shall we?'

Together they went downstairs, just as Simonie was hanging up the receiver. 'That was a couple I couldn't reach yesterday,' he said. 'Mr and Mrs Richards. They're still coming on the trip, so at least I won't have to cancel it altogether!'

'That's terrific!' said Mandy.

'But . . . it definitely means there'll be no room for you two,' Simonie said. 'I'm sorry.'

Adam Hope shrugged his shoulders. 'Don't be. There are still lots of things for us to see here in Kimmirut – right, Mandy?'

Mandy smiled and nodded. Just then there was a knock at the back door, and Simonie went off to answer it.

Mandy and Mr Hope followed him through to the kitchen. A burly man in warm, expensive-looking clothes was standing in the doorway.

'Dad, it's the man who was talking to Mr Tupilak at the race,' Mandy whispered.

Adam Hope nodded. 'So it is.'

'My name's Tom Ellison,' the man was saying. 'Hope you don't mind me calling round like this so early, but I'm here on business.'

'Business?' Simonie echoed politely.

'I hear you've got a sled-trip organised for today? I'd like to book three places, please.'

Mandy clutched her dad's arm. 'Three of them, two of us . . . with five to a sled . . .'

Simonie turned round to Mandy and Adam Hope with a surprised smile. 'Well, if you two still want to come on this trip . . .'

Adam Hope grinned. 'Count us in!'

'Then, Mr Ellison, I can certainly take your booking!' Simonie said happily.

Mandy cheered and hugged her dad.

Mr Ellison didn't seem to notice them.

'I know it's short notice,' he went on to Simonie. 'I *had* booked a place with that guy Thomas Tupilak. But now I've seen your dogs are faster, I reckon we should travel with you.' He smiled briefly. 'I like to have the best of everything.'

Simonie went through the arrangements for the trip. Then he waved Mr Ellison goodbye and turned back to Mandy and her dad, a broad grin on his face.

Mr Hope shook Simonie warmly by the hand. 'That's fantastic news for your business!'

'We leave at eleven o'clock this morning,' said Simonie.

'I'll tell your mum that we'll be off,' Adam Hope called to Mandy as he headed upstairs.

'And I'll tell Pani,' Mandy replied, her eyes shining as she grabbed her padded winter coat from the porch. 'This is going to be the best trip ever!'

* * *

Out in the dog yard, Mandy saw that Pani had put out breakfast for the dogs and was now putting leads on a jostling crowd of small puppies.

'Hi, Mandy!' she called. 'How are you this morning?'

'Great!' Mandy shouted back. 'I'm going to be keeping you company on the sled-trip! Some more people are joining the trip.'

'That's fantastic,' Pani said with a big smile. 'You won't believe the things you'll see!'

Just then Mandy saw Nanook's head poke out from her kennel. Sniffing the air, she turned to look at them. The door to her pen was open, so she trotted out to greet Mandy, her tail wagging behind her.

Mandy beamed and crouched down in the snow to fuss the husky. 'Will Nanook be coming on the trip?' she asked Pani.

Pani nodded. 'Leading the team, as usual. I'll make sure we get to ride on her sled!'

Mandy put her face close to Nanook's

warm, dog-scented fur. 'A real Arctic sled-trip,' she whispered to the beautiful husky. 'I can't wait!'

'Everything packed?' asked Adam Hope as Mandy emerged from her bedroom at half-past ten. She nodded, then saw her dad stare at the bulging sports bag she was dragging behind her. 'Er, when I said *"everything"*. . .' he began, raising his eyebrows.

'I haven't packed *that* much!' Mandy protested. 'How's Mum feeling?'

'Well, she's turned quite a funny shade,' Mr Hope said, but his concerned face soon brightened into a broad smile. 'Green with envy!'

Mandy smiled despite herself, as she went to say goodbye to her mum.

'Ready to go?' Emily Hope asked. She was propped up in bed with a box of tissues, her voice thick and croaky. 'I wish I was going with you.'

Mandy gave her mum a hug. 'I wish you were too.'

Mrs Hope hugged her back. 'Take care, Mandy. And look after your dad!'

'I will,' Mandy promised. 'Something tells me this trip's going to be one to remember!'

As Mandy walked outside, Simonie was discussing something in Inuktitut with a man who was crouched over one of the sleds. 'Adam, Mandy, meet your driver, Gaborik,' Simonie said.

'Hey, good to meet you!' Gaborik called in a deep voice. He was only a couple of centimetres taller than Mandy, but he looked stocky and strong – almost like a husky, Mandy thought to herself. His long, black hair was untidily plaited and his brown eyes twinkled as he took their bags. 'I've just been cleaning and checking the sled,' he explained.

'Are we ready to go, Dad?' asked Pani, coming up behind them with her own bag.

'I've told everybody we'll meet at the Park Centre,' Simonie replied. 'I'll lead the way.'

They set off in good spirits along the main road. There were six dogs in harness pulling each of the two large sleds. The drivers called out commands, and the dogs obeyed without hesitation. Mandy, her dad and Pani were in Gaborik's sled. Simonie drove the other sled, which was empty and ready for the tourists.

The sun was out, making the snowy verges glisten and sparkle. Mandy saw the light catch on something around Pani's neck, and looked more closely. 'That's a beautiful necklace,' she said, studying the little rose-coloured stones set into long loops of silver.

Pani smiled. 'Thank you. My mother made it. She makes a lot of jewellery, and sells it in town.'

'What are those stones?' Mandy asked. 'They're lovely.'

Pani nodded proudly. 'They're pieces of red apatite. It's a kind of crystal. You'll find lots of pretty stones in the ground around here.'

'I'll keep a look out,' said Mandy. Then something else caught her eye. 'What's that?' she asked, pointing to a stone pillar rising up from the snow by the side of the road.

'*Innuksuk*,' said Gaborik, as if this explained everything.

Adam Hope raised his eyebrows at Pani.

'One of the ancient markers built by our people to help them find their way around the island,' she told him. 'There are many inside the park too.'

'I'm pleased to hear we won't get lost then,' Mr Hope said. 'In *any* language!'

Soon the Katannilik Park Centre came into view. As the sleds drew closer, Mandy could see a couple of taxis and a big red truck parked outside. Some of the tourists had already arrived and were waiting for them.

'You're ten minutes late,' Mr Ellison complained gruffly as they approached. 'You told me eleven o'clock, Mr Nanogak.'

'It doesn't matter, Tom,' said a slim woman beside him who somehow managed to look glamorous even in her dark green anorak and waterproof trousers. 'Don't fuss.'

'I'm not fussing, Julie,' Mr Ellison protested. 'But if the man says he's going to be here at eleven . . .'

'I apologise if you've been waiting,'

Simonie said quickly. 'Hopefully the other tourists will arrive soon. In the meantime, let me help you load your things.'

'I hope this thing's safe,' said a man standing with the Ellisons. He had thinning blond hair and a bushy moustache.

'It's very comfortable, actually,' said Mandy's dad, offering his hand to shake. 'I'm Adam Hope, by the way.'

The man took his hand and shook it firmly. 'Ben Page.' He nodded to Mr Ellison. 'Tom's business partner. Just got here from Toronto.'

Julie Ellison flashed a dazzling smile at Mandy. 'Where are you from, honey?' she asked.

Mandy smiled back. 'We're from England.'

Julie Ellison looked interested. 'How lovely. I wanted to take a vacation in England, but Tom *insisted* we come and freeze to death here . . .'

'Well, never mind that now,' said Tom

Ellison briskly, climbing into the sled and leaving his luggage on the ground for someone else to deal with. 'Are we going or what?' He pointed at a big caribou logo on the side of the building. 'I'm itching to see one of those for real.'

But as Gaborik heaved the Ellisons' luggage into the back of their sled, Mandy felt her blood run suddenly cold.

The zip of one holdall had come undone. And inside she could see the cold grey metal of a hunting rifle.

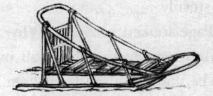

Four

'Dad,' Mandy hissed, pointing at the holdall. 'Dad, *look*!'

Immediately Mr Hope stood up and tapped on Simonie's shoulder.

'You seem to have packed some interesting luggage, Mr Ellison,' Simonie Nanogak said calmly.

'What? The gun?' Tom Ellison said, looking surprised. 'What about it?'

Mandy saw that Simonie's eyes had

narrowed. 'Hunting is forbidden in the park,' he said sternly.

Ben Page looked puzzled. 'Why? Those caribou are wandering about all over the place. There are thousands of them.'

'We like to preserve our wildlife here,' Simonie said.

'Hey, don't get uptight,' Mr Ellison retorted. 'Ben was just joking. Right, Ben?'

'Sure,' Ben Page said quickly.

Gaborik had been checking in the other tourists. Now he had come over to see what was going on. Like Simonie, he didn't seem amused. 'We don't kill the wildlife just for our amusement.'

'Right . . . whatever,' the burly Canadian said with a tight smile. 'OK, so we won't be using our rifles while we're on this trip.'

'Thank you,' said Simonie. As he spoke, a yellow taxi-cab pulled up in the car park. A warmly dressed, middle-aged couple got out and Simonie waved to them. 'Ah, here's Mr and Mrs Richards.'

'Then we're all here,' Gaborik said. 'We can set off when you're ready.'

Simonie nodded. 'Good. I'll go and help them with their luggage.' With a last glance at Mr Ellison, he walked off to the cab.

Mr Hope smiled at Mandy. 'That's that sorted out, then,' he muttered. But Mandy noticed Mr Ellison wink at Ben Page as he climbed aboard. The two men started whispering together, although Mandy couldn't hear what they were saying.

'Don't worry, Mandy,' said Pani beside her in a low voice. 'Dad won't let them do any harm.'

'I suppose not,' Mandy agreed. She decided to take her mind off the two Canadians by looking at the tourists boarding the other sled instead. Mr and Mrs Richards climbed in behind a young couple and another man. Mrs Richards caught her eye and smiled as she settled into her seat, and Mandy grinned back.

Just then, Nanook barked noisily, clearly eager to be off. Watching the huskies move restlessly in the harness, Mandy felt a sudden thrill of excitement.

Then Gaborik shouted a command and Nanook strained against the reins, leading the husky team away, out of the frozen car park and on to the snowy road. Mr Hope, sitting in front, clapped his gloved hands together, and a cheer went up from the sled that Simonie was driving, following on behind.

Pani squeezed Mandy's arm as their sled picked up speed. 'Here we go!' It was a bit of a squash in their sled, as three tourists made a cargo of seven in total, but Mandy was glad of the extra warmth she got from sitting so close to Pani.

Tourists browsing outside shop windows watched them go by and waved. Mr Hope waved back and turned to grin at Mandy. 'Do you suppose this is what the Queen feels like when she drives through London?' he joked.

Mandy laughed. 'She'd have to swap her corgies for huskies!'

As they pulled away from town, fewer houses lined the streets. A snowplough rumbled past in the opposite direction, and Gaborik exchanged a cheery wave with the driver. As its engine died away in the distance, a hush fell over the frozen land. The sled tracks hissed as the party carried on towards the park. The dogs ran eagerly along behind Nanook in silence, letting nothing distract them from the road ahead. Soon Kimmirut was far behind them, just a dark smudge against the snow.

Mandy settled back and gazed around. The flat white wilderness seemed to stretch on for ever, interrupted by clumps of Arctic heather or dwarf willows. Then the sleds pulled into a broad valley that rose and fell in great white sweeps around an emerald-green river. This was the entrance to the Katannilik National Park.

'That's the Soper River,' Pani said. 'Isn't it beautiful?'

'It's *all* beautiful,' Mandy answered simply.

'I've come here so many times,' said Pani, 'but each time I imagine I'm the first person to find it.'

'Don't take anything for granted in the park,' Gaborik announced. 'The *Tuniit* roam this land.'

'What are the Tuniit?' asked Julie Ellison.

'The people who lived here when the Inuit first came to the island,' Gaborik replied, narrowing his eyes against the icy wind as they sped on across the snow.

'Ah,' said Tom Ellison, winking at Mr Page. 'Ghosts, you mean.'

Gaborik shrugged. 'If you like. They had great strength and stamina. Legends say they slept with their feet above their heads to make them better runners. The elders say they have seen them moving across the hills in groups, dressed in caribou skins.'

Mandy smiled at her dad. It was a good story.

'You're giving me the creeps,' complained Mrs Ellison, who suddenly looked quite pale.

'Oh, come on, Julie,' her husband protested. 'A bunch of things in the distance that look like caribou? I reckon that'll be a herd of caribou!'

Ben Page joined him in noisy laughter. Mandy looked worriedly at Gaborik, afraid he might be offended, but he simply smiled and turned back to the track.

They journeyed on, the huskies churning up the pristine snow of the hillside and showing no sign of tiring even when the slope got steeper. Beside them, some way below, the Soper curled and twisted along until it fell away into what looked like clouds of spray.

'A waterfall!' Mandy exclaimed.

'That's what Katannilik means,' Pani told her quietly with a smile, staring at the frothing water. 'The place of waterfalls.'

'What's that?' asked Adam Hope suddenly, as they reached the brow of the hill and the land levelled out. Mandy saw he was looking away from the river, craning his neck to see something in the distance. 'Over there . . .'

Mandy followed his gaze. She could just make out a large black smear over the frosted ground. It looked horribly out of place amid the thick white drifts.

'Simonie is going to investigate,' Gaborik announced, as the other sled changed its course to pass nearer to the dark circle. Mandy jumped as Gaborik gave a new order to the dogs and they followed on, the huskies racing even faster after their kennel companions.

As they approached the ugly black stain on the landscape, Mandy realised what they were looking at. 'Ashes!' she exclaimed.

'Someone's been having a campfire,' her dad agreed.

'It's illegal to start a fire outside a designated camp area,' Gaborik said gravely.

Adam Hope frowned. 'Whoever it was seems to have had quite a party, by the looks of things.'

As they got closer they could see there was rubbish strewn all around the area. Crushed drink cans lay beside empty crisp packets and discarded boxes. Plastic bags, blown by the wind, rustled and scuttled about the scorched circle like strange animals.

'Some picnic,' Mandy muttered as the sled slowed to a halt. Simonie was already off the sled, shaking his head sadly as Gaborik crossed to join him. The dogs stood waiting in silence, looking about with pricked ears and panting out steam into the cold air.

'How could anyone do this?' Mandy had spotted the butchered stumps of some nearby willows, their branches twisted off and used, she guessed, as fuel for the fire. 'There are so few trees here to begin with. It's . . . it's so *thoughtless*. Spoiling this lovely place for everyone.'

'Sure, it's lovely here,' Mr Ellison piped up impatiently. 'So it seems to me we're wasting our time looking at a pile of rubbish!'

Mr Hope nodded in agreement. 'You're quite right.'

Mandy looked at him, amazed. 'Dad!'

'We *are* wasting time just looking at this mess,' he went on. 'We should be helping to clear it up. Coming?' He jumped to his feet and climbed out.

Mr Ellison scowled and looked away. Mandy hid her smile and scrambled out of the sled to join her dad. Julie Ellison shifted in her seat uncomfortably, but only Pani followed them into the snow.

Simonie smiled gratefully as they started to collect the litter, their fingers made clumsy by the thick gloves they wore.

'Who's responsible for all this, do you think?' Mandy asked.

Gaborik looked meaningfully at Simonie. 'Who else runs sled-trips out into the park?' he said.

'Thomas Tupilak,' Simonie muttered darkly.

'The nearest shelter is not far away,' Gaborik growled as he grabbed again for a carrier bag that kept blowing out of reach. 'Why would tourists want to make such a mess here, in the open?'

Suddenly a high, keening noise rang out. It echoed around the valley, a long wailing howl, followed soon after by another. Mandy straightened up and looked around in alarm, but the valley seemed empty. By the sleds, the huskies began to shift about and some of them whined uneasily. Only Nanook stood stock still, a little way apart from the other dogs as usual, her pointed ears pricked up, listening intently to the eerie call.

'What was that noise?' Mandy asked.

'Wolves,' Simonie answered quietly. 'Many of them. And by the sound of it, quite close by.'

Five

A startled burst of chatter started up among the tourists as another wolf howl echoed round the valley. Mandy saw Mrs Ellison clutch hold of her husband's arm in alarm. Tom Ellison looked a bit anxious himself.

'Could these picnic remains have attracted them?' Adam Hope wondered.

'It's possible,' Simonie agreed. 'A wolf has an incredible sense of smell.'

'You'd better get us out of here!' said Ben Page nervously.

Pani nudged Mandy. 'Doesn't he know that wolves don't attack people?' she whispered with a mischievous grin.

'Mr Page is right, we should go,' Simonie said. 'We'll head for the camp lodge at the valley mouth as planned. Then I'll come back and clear up this mess properly.'

Pani looked worried. 'It'll be getting dark soon, Dad.'

'Don't worry, Pani.' Simonie placed a hand on her shoulder and smiled. 'It's not too far to the lodge, and I'll have the dogs with me.'

Nanook barked at them, as if joining in the discussion. Now the wolf cries had died away she seemed impatient to be off again. Mandy ruffled her fur affectionately, marvelling again at how brilliantly it kept the dogs warm and dry.

'What if the wolves are here when you come back?' Mr Hope asked Simonie.

'You'll be glad we brought our guns along, after all, right?' Mr Ellison called.

Simonie shook his head. 'No, no,' he said, sounding a little impatient. 'They shouldn't bother us. In any case, we have flare guns. The noise and light will scare away any curious wolves that might get too near.'

'I'll come too,' said Mr Hope.

'Thanks,' Simonie said. 'We'll be glad of your help.'

'Please can we go now?' Mrs Ellison cried shakily, staring all around as if expecting a wolf to sneak up on her at any moment. Mandy caught Pani's eye and grinned. It looked like these tourists weren't quite ready to face *all* the wildlife in the park.

'Come on, Mandy.' Gaborik smiled at her. 'It's warm in the lodge. You won't have to wait for us for long.'

Mandy nodded, and climbed back in next to Pani. Gaborik shouted an order at the dogs and their sled lurched forward, away

from the remains of the campfire, towards
their home for the night.

Daylight was fading as they reached the
lodge. Mandy checked her watch – it was
nearly three o'clock. The lodge looked like a
large wooden cabin. A cheer went up from
the tourists as it came into view.

'There you are, Mandy,' said Mr Hope.
'Home sweet home for the Arctic trekker.'

'Perfect!' Mandy breathed a sigh of relief.
'I can't wait to get out of the cold!'

The dogs slowed down as they approached
the lodge, without Gaborik or Simonie
needing to say a word. Mandy guessed they
were well-used to this routine. Once the sleds
were parked outside, the huskies waited
patiently, panting clouds of steam into the
cold air.

'Sorry guys,' Gaborik told the dogs,
scratching Saliq behind the ear. 'Work's not
over just yet!'

Simonie started to help everyone out of the sleds and Gaborik lifted out the luggage.

'Come on, Mandy,' said Pani, clambering over the side of their sled. 'Let's get inside.'

'Does anyone live here permanently at the lodge?' Mandy asked.

'No, the tour parties are left to look after themselves,' Pani explained as they reached the front door.

Mandy pushed her gloved hands against the dark wood, and the door swung open. 'Hey, it's not locked!' she exclaimed.

Mr Hope strode up behind her. 'Nothing to steal, I suppose. And open to everyone!'

The door led to a large room whose walls were lined with wooden chairs and a couple of old but comfy-looking settees. Pani ran over to a grey metal box on the wall, stamping snow all over the rough wooden floorboards.

'Heating!' Mandy cried, her eyes lighting up.

Pani grinned and flicked on the switch. 'We'll soon warm up now!'

'Thanks, honey,' Mrs Ellison said gratefully as she walked inside. 'I can't feel my fingers or toes at all! For all I know, they could have fallen off.' She looked around the room unhappily. 'It's a bit basic, isn't it?'

Tom Ellison nodded. 'Too right, honey!'

'Oh, it's not that bad,' said Mr Richards, looking round appreciatively as he stood in the doorway. 'And look, there's a radio, too.'

'The sleeping quarters are through there,' Gaborik said, coming into the main room and pointing to a partition in the far wall. He pushed open a door beside him. 'And this is the kitchen. The back door leads to the washrooms.'

Mrs Ellison's mouth fell open in shock. 'You mean the bathrooms aren't *en suite*?'

Mandy caught Pani's eye and the two of them had to stifle their laughter.

Simonie gave her a sympathetic smile. 'I'm

sure you'll be fine, Mrs Ellison. Do make yourselves comfortable, everyone. Pani, perhaps you could make some tea and heat some soup for our guests while we are gone?'

Pani nodded and went into the kitchen. Mandy followed her through. A few minutes later she peered through the kitchen window and saw the two sleds gliding away into the distance.

'Why have they taken both sleds?' Mandy asked.

'So they didn't have to waste time bedding down half the dogs before they went,' said Pani as she started gathering mugs from a cupboard. 'They'll be back before you know it, you'll see.'

The soup and tea went down well with everyone. Afterwards, while the tourists sat around in the warm cabin swapping camping stories, Mandy and Pani sat by the window. Their warm breath misted up the glass, which gave Mandy an idea. They each took turns to draw animal pictures on the pane with their fingers. Then the other had to guess what the animal was.

Pani's latest picture was puzzling Mandy. 'Er – is it an otter?'

'No, silly!' laughed Pani. 'It's a lemming!'

'But I've never seen a lemming!' Mandy protested, laughing too.

'I'm not surprised,' said Pani. 'They move

like lightning. But maybe if we're lucky we might get to see one tomorrow. They breed really quickly in the summer, and to make sure there's enough for them all to eat in winter, they spread all over the park – thousands of them!'

'Wow,' grinned Mandy. 'I really hope we see one . . .'

Just then she trailed off, distracted by a raised voice in the kitchen. Glancing through the half-closed door she saw Tom and Julie Ellison glaring at each other, clearly having some kind of argument.

'Why is this so important to you?' Mandy heard Mrs Ellison say.

'Ben and I came here to relax,' her husband said grumpily. 'Getting away from it all! Nothing but hunting and fishing . . .'

'Isn't it enough just to *watch* the wildlife? It's my holiday too!' came Julie Ellison's angry reply.

'And who's paying for it?' hissed Tom

Ellison. 'Me! I just want my money's worth, that's all.' He pulled out a tiny mobile phone.

'Just don't get any stupid ideas in your head, Tom Ellison,' his wife warned him.

Mandy frowned. She didn't feel comfortable eavesdropping, but she was glad Mrs Ellison didn't seem to care much for her husband's bloodthirsty hobbies. 'Come on,' she told Pani, wiping away the lemming and steaming up the glass again with some quick breaths. 'My turn!'

Mandy was just in the middle of drawing a caribou's antlers when two distant yellow lights shone through the window.

'They're back!' Mandy cried, her eyes shining.

'Come on,' Pani said. 'Let's go and meet them!'

Quickly throwing on their coats, scarves and gloves, they took a torch and went into the kitchen. Mrs Ellison smiled at them as they walked past her to the back door, though she looked worried. Mandy frowned. Where had Mr Ellison gone?

Together, she and Pani stepped out into the frozen darkness to greet the sleds. Mandy played the powerful torch-beam about the area. 'Where will the dogs be staying?' she asked.

'We normally bed them down on the tent platforms, where people pitch their tents in the summer,' Pani explained, shining her own torch on to what looked like a number of wide flat steps leading up the rocky hillside. 'There are poles and chains to keep the dogs secured. They're sheltered by windbreaks, too, so the bedding Dad's brought along won't blow away.'

Suddenly there was a movement behind them. Mandy jumped as the kitchen door opened. She was relieved to see it was only Tom Ellison going back inside. He was slipping his mobile phone back into his pocket.

If he wanted to make a call, why didn't he make it inside? Mandy wondered. Just then, the howling and barking of the approaching huskies got louder, and the sleds pulled up with a hiss beside them. She and Pani cheered with delight.

'This is a nice, warm welcome!' exclaimed Adam Hope, a large bag full of rubbish perched on his lap. 'Just the job in weather like this!'

'The litter has all been cleared away,' Gaborik said. He looked tired but satisfied. 'Did you save some soup for us?'

'Of course,' said Mandy. 'There's plenty inside. Did you see any wolves?'

Adam Hope shook his head, scattering snow from his beard and the fur-lined hood of his coat. 'No. We heard a few of them in the hills, but nothing came to bother us.'

'With this bunch of dogs about I'm not surprised,' smiled Mandy. While Pani gave Nanook a special welcome, Mandy crouched down to fuss Okpik and all the others. The huskies snuffled playfully around in the snow, sensing that work was over for the day.

'Would you and Mandy like to start bedding the dogs down for the night, Pani?' Simonie said. 'We'll warm up a little and mix the dogs' meat ration.'

'OK,' Mandy said as Pani rushed for the box of dog supplies on the sled. Mandy followed her friend, the dogs jumping up and nudging at her legs with their noses.

It didn't take them long to unpack the rolls of bedding and water dishes and lead each husky to its overnight home. Mandy was cold and tired when she came back inside with Pani, but it was good to know that the dogs were safe and warm, nestled together on the tent platform beneath the cover of a thick tarpaulin.

Her dad greeted them in the kitchen. 'That's the dogs made comfortable for the night,' he observed. 'Now it's your turn!

Through to the bedroom, girls, it's time to choose bunks!'

'I'll have one next to Mandy,' Pani said instantly.

'I thought you'd say that,' grinned Mr Hope. 'There are still two together at the far end.'

'Great!' Mandy said, pulling off her heavy coat and smoothing back her hair from her face.

The communal bedroom was filled with bunk beds, each pair kept separate by wooden screens for privacy. Pani went over to the two beds at the far end against the wall. 'This is the best spot,' she explained. 'No one walks past you in the night! Top bunk or bottom?'

'Bottom, please,' Mandy answered with a loud yawn. She tested the thin mattress under the rough blankets. It couldn't have been more different from her soft, comfy bed back home, and yet she wouldn't have swapped it for the world. 'This is the best trip ever,' she told Pani. 'I'm so glad we could come!'

'Wait till we reach the plateau tomorrow,' Pani told her. 'The caribou love it, you'll see lots of them there.'

But the thought of seeing lots of caribou filled Mandy with worry. 'I hope Mr Ellison and his friend will leave them alone.'

Pani frowned. 'They'll be on the sled with us, won't they? What can they do with our dads around?'

Mandy forced a smile. 'I know, you're right,' she said.

But after dinner that night, lying in bed in the dark, she couldn't stop thinking about Tom Ellison. Why had Mrs Ellison seemed so upset? Mandy tried to let the muffled chatter and laughter of the adults in the room next door lull her to sleep, but questions kept crowding her head.

Mandy only realised she'd fallen asleep

when she was woken by a clattering noise. 'Pani,' she whispered. 'Pani, did you hear that?' But there was only soft snoring from the bunk above her.

Mandy tried to go back to sleep but she was convinced she could hear something – or some*one* – outside. She thought about waking her dad, but she wasn't sure she could find the right bunk in the pitch blackness.

She lay there in the dark, trying to decide what to do. Then, she quickly pulled her jeans over her pyjamas and crept along the length of the dormitory to the door.

The living room beyond was also in darkness. The only light came through the window, where the pale moonlight bathed the snowy wastes outside in an eerie glow. As Mandy padded towards the kitchen, she heard another clattering noise. Her heart leaped. Someone was definitely out there!

Six

Mandy was opening the kitchen door to investigate when a hand came down heavily on her shoulder. She was about to cry out in surprise when she recognised the low voice in her ear.

'It's me, Mandy,' Simonie said softly. 'I'm sorry to have scared you.'

Mandy gave a sigh of relief. 'What are you doing out here?'

'The same as you, I imagine,' said Mr

Nanogak. 'I heard noises. Sorry to creep up on you, but I didn't think you'd want to miss this.'

'Miss what?' asked Mandy.

'I saw him at the living room window,' Simonie whispered. 'Then I heard you in the kitchen. If you'd opened the door you'd have frightened him away.' He wiped some condensation from the window and pointed. Now Mandy could see a small pale shape trotting about outside over the moonlit snow.

'What is it?' Mandy whispered, not daring to move.

'An Arctic fox,' Simonie murmured. 'They're very shy animals; it's not often you'll see one up close.'

Mandy held her breath as the Arctic fox came a little closer. She had seen a red fox darting over the ice of the frozen Hudson Bay, but that had been from up high in a helicopter. Now she couldn't believe her luck, seeing such a beautiful animal up close.

It was similar in size and shape to a collie dog, but its ears were short and pointed, and its fur was almost silver.

'He must have smelt the leftovers from our dinner,' Simonie said softly. 'The clattering we heard was him pushing the lid off the dustbin.'

Mandy could see the fox burying its long snout in a bundle of tin foil, snapping at the chicken scraps inside. It looked from side to side as if checking it was still alone, then lifted its head and stared through the window, straight at Mandy. She didn't even breathe for fear of scaring their timid visitor.

Suddenly there was a familiar howl from outside.

Mandy recognised it at once. 'Quiet, Nanook!' she whispered, but another bark echoed out of the darkness.

'The dogs have picked up foxy's scent,' Simonie told her. 'He won't risk staying any longer.'

Sure enough, the fox swiftly lowered its head, grabbed the tin foil and darted away into the shadows of the night. One more bark sounded from the dogs' enclosure. Then there was silence.

'That was amazing,' Mandy said, grinning up at Simonie. 'Thanks for stopping me when you did!'

'I'm just glad we found out who was making the noise.' Simonie yawned.

Mandy found herself yawning too. 'Well, I'm glad I got up. I wouldn't have missed that for anything.' Just as she was about to turn from the window, she noticed fluffy white flakes drifting down from the indigo sky. 'Snow! Will the huskies be OK out there?'

Simonie smiled kindly. 'Don't worry. The tarpaulin will keep them dry and they have each other for warmth.' He gestured to the sleeping quarters. 'Well, that's enough excitement for one night, I think. Who knows what we'll see tomorrow?'

Mandy went back to bed full of happy, drowsy dreams of what the morning would bring.

When she woke, it was to the sound of anxious voices, and heavy boots striding back and forth across the wooden floors. Mandy rubbed her eyes and got up. Pani's bed was empty. She frowned. It wasn't long after dawn. Surely she wasn't the last to wake?

Then the door opened and Pani came into the room. She ran up to Mandy, her face tense with worry.

'What's up?' Mandy asked, suddenly wide awake. She let Pani lead her silently past the rows of bunks. Behind the partitions she could hear the other tourists stirring, talking in low puzzled voices.

'Look,' said Pani simply, when they reached the bunks closest to the door. Her brown eyes were full of concern.

Mandy frowned. 'Two empty beds?' Then her stomach twisted as she realised who must have been sleeping there. 'Tom Ellison and Ben Page?' she breathed, looking at Pani with wide, fearful eyes.

Pani nodded solemnly. 'And they've taken their guns!'

Mandy rushed into the living room, and found her dad and Simonie already dressed. Mr Hope gave them both a fleeting smile, but Mandy could see the anxiety in his eyes.

Julie Ellison, who looked very pale without her make-up on, was curled in a chair, wearing a pair of fleecy blue pyjamas. 'I'm really sorry,' she said. 'All I can tell you is, they've gone!'

Mr Nanogak smiled at her sympathetically. 'We know they've gone, and not just for a walk either, since their luggage is missing too. But *where* have they gone? Why would they just leave like this?'

Mrs Ellison shrugged helplessly. 'Tom and Ben just decided the trip ... well ...' She shook her head, close to tears. 'I guess they thought that maybe they would make their own way through the park.'

'The fools!' Simonie turned away. 'The park can be a dangerous place when you don't know your way around. If they get lost, or caught in bad weather . . .'

'When did they leave?' Adam Hope asked more gently.

'I'm not sure.' Mrs Ellison knit her fingers together nervously. 'Maybe an hour or two ago?'

'While they're on this trip, I'm responsible for their safety. We have to find them,' Simonie said firmly. 'Gaborik should be able to pick up their trail.'

Right on cue, the door crashed open, letting a blast of icy air into the room. Gaborik swiftly closed it behind him, and shook his head. 'Not a sign of them,' he reported. 'But there are tyre marks at the end of the track . . . someone must have picked them up.'

Adam Hope frowned. 'But who would come all the way out here, at this hour of the morning?'

Mandy turned to Pani, suddenly excited. 'Last night, when you were showing me the tent platform, do you remember what we saw?' She swung round to Mrs Ellison. 'You were talking in the kitchen, then Mr Ellison went outside to make a call on his mobile phone. You . . .' She paused, not wanting to seem rude. 'You didn't seem very pleased.'

'Is this true?' Simonie asked Mrs Ellison quietly.

She nodded. 'He said he wanted to get his money's worth from this holiday. He wanted to go hunting and fishing, and if you wouldn't let him he'd find someone who would.'

'And we all know who that is, don't we?' Gaborik said darkly. 'Who else would drive all the way out here in the night at the sniff of an easy dollar?'

Pani sighed. 'Thomas Tupilak.'

Simonie looked hard at Mrs Ellison. 'I told your husband and his friend before that it's a criminal offence to go hunting in the park. The authorities will take this very seriously. We must stop them before they do any harm, either to the park or themselves.'

'Can't we phone up Thomas Tupilak?' Adam Hope suggested. 'Try to make them all see sense?'

'Good idea.' Simonie pulled out his mobile and started dialling. 'I know his number. I've seen it on his fancy brochures enough times.'

Everyone waited in a tense silence. Gaborik started pacing the room like a caged animal, his long plaited hair tossing about like a tail. But a minute or so later, Simonie angrily hung up. 'No answer.' Then he peered at his phone's display. 'And that's all we need – the batteries are running low. I'd better turn this thing off for now.'

'So now what?' asked Mandy in desperation.

'Are you going to go after them, Dad?' asked Pani.

Simonie sighed noisily. 'I don't see I have much choice. Like I said, they signed up for the sled-trip so they're my responsibility. I'll have to go after them.'

'But they could be anywhere in the park,' Gaborik protested. 'Tupilak must be travelling by truck. It'll take us much longer by sled.'

Simonie nodded and turned again to Julie Ellison. 'Did your husband give you any idea where he was going?'

The woman thought hard. 'I don't think so . . .' Then she brightened, and Mandy felt a surge of hope. 'Wait! I heard him and Ben talking about a waterfall.'

There was an awkward silence.

'There are many waterfalls in the park,' Gaborik told her stiffly.

'Anything else?' prompted Adam Hope.

Mrs Ellison shook her head helplessly. 'I remember he and Ben kept saying something about having an . . . *appetite* for caribou. Again and again, like it was real funny.' She sniffed. 'It didn't make *me* laugh.'

Mandy shuddered and turned away. Pani looked down at the floor.

'Wait a moment,' said Simonie. 'I know an area upland from here, where there are many caribou at this time of year. They go there because the wind blows the ground free of snow, uncovering the lichens for them to eat. And there is a large waterfall nearby.'

Mr Hope scratched his chin. 'Sounds a likely spot to me,' he said.

'Let's go,' said Gaborik. 'I'll get the dogs ready.'

'No, Gaborik,' Simonie told him. '*I'll* go. You must stay here and look after the rest of our party.' Gaborik opened his mouth to protest but Simonie raised a hand to stop him. 'No arguments, there isn't time. The sled-trip will have to be postponed for now. Everyone will have to stay here until this mess is sorted out.'

'I'm so sorry,' said Mrs Ellison.

Simonie shrugged. 'Hopefully we'll be underway again soon.'

'Let me come with you,' said Adam Hope. 'Hopefully we'll arrive in time to avoid any trouble, but you could find wounded animals out there. If you do, you'll need me.'

Simonie considered for a moment, then nodded. 'All right. Thank you, Adam.'

'I'll come with you too,' Mandy said immediately.

'Oh no you won't, love!' Mr Hope shook his head. 'You'll stay here where it's safe.'

'But . . .' Mandy bit her tongue. She could see it was useless to argue. The best thing she could do was let them get on without any fuss. There was no time to waste. 'Good luck, Dad,' she murmured, giving him a hug. 'Be careful.'

Pani gently squeezed her arm as they went back into the sleeping quarters to get dressed. 'They'll only be taking one sled,' she pointed out. 'We can exercise the other dogs till they come back.'

For Pani's sake, Mandy forced a smile. 'Good idea,' she said, fishing under her bunk for her rucksack and yanking out some clean clothes. 'Last one dressed has to make breakfast!'

But while Mandy, Pani and the dogs ran around all morning, the time only crawled by. For what felt like the hundredth time, Mandy checked her watch. It was approaching eleven o'clock. Her father and Mr Nanogak had been gone for three hours.

Gaborik had taken the rest of the tourists on a short walk around the area, though the deep, crisp snow didn't make hiking very easy. Now they were all sitting inside the lodge waiting for news. Mrs Ellison was lying down in the sleeping quarters, staying out of the way of the others.

Mandy watched Saliq, Sedna and the other huskies at play, madly sprinting about without a care in the world. She supposed they were just like any other working animals, like guide dogs or police dogs – the harnesses were their uniform, and told them it was time to work. When the harnesses came off it was time to play.

But Nanook didn't seem interested in playing with the others. She seemed quite happy just sniffing around near the kitchen door.

'I bet she can smell that fox you saw last night,' said Pani.

Mandy nodded. Nanook raised her head and looked about keenly. Her pale blue eyes settled on Mandy for a moment. Then she trotted over and sat at Mandy's feet. The two girls fussed and stroked her.

'Your grandad calls Nanook a lone wolf,' Mandy said thoughtfully.

'Well, I hope she's the only kind of wolf we'll meet out here!' said Pani.

Mandy smiled. 'It's a good description, though, isn't it? She looks even more like a wolf than the other dogs do.' She looked admiringly at Nanook's lean frame and long slender legs. Her face was more pointed than usual for a husky, and her white coat seemed longer and thicker.

'She's beautiful,' said Pani fondly, and Mandy nodded in agreement.

A sudden, loud bark made Mandy jump. 'Okpik!' she cried, finding the small dog beside her. He was panting hard, but soon raced off again, apparently determined not to waste a moment of his surprise day off. When he saw Mandy wasn't following, he bounded back up to her, barked and ran away again, hoping she would get the hang of his game.

'Oh dear, Mandy,' said Pani, stroking the curled tip of Nanook's ear. 'Looks like you're not doing well in Okpik's human obedience class!'

Hearing his name, the wiry dog raced back over and barked at them, his dark eyes pleading for attention. 'All right, I give in,' Mandy said, setting off after him. He sped away even faster than before, haring up a slope and round behind her in an enormous circle, snow scattering up from his paws. She chased after him for a bit, but soon got tired, tramping through the deep snow.

Seeing that Mandy had stopped running, Nanook got up and left Pani's side. She came up to Mandy and lifted a paw.

'All that playing with Okpik has made her jealous,' Pani teased. 'She wants some attention. I've never seen her make such a fuss of any visitor!'

Mandy felt very pleased. 'Really?' She crouched down beside Nanook and took the offered paw. 'You've not got another stone stuck in there, have you?' She checked, but Nanook's paw was fine. The husky licked Mandy's wrist as if to thank her for looking.

Just then something high above Mandy caught her eye. It was a hawk, circling in the white sky. There was something ominous about the large bird soaring silently above. Hawks were birds of prey. Had it spied a wounded animal nearby? Was it hungrily keeping watch? Like Mr Ellison, the bird might have an appetite for caribou too . . .

Mandy shivered, and stamped her feet up and down in an effort to warm herself up. Mr Ellison's words echoed through her mind again and again. *Appetite for caribou* . . . Why had he and Ben Page found that so funny? Like it was a joke . . .

'Hey, you two!' Gaborik was calling them

from the back doorway. 'I'm making tea. Want some?'

Mandy shook her head. 'No thanks,' she called.

'The dogs are warming us up enough right now!' Pani added.

'Has Dad called in?' asked Mandy.

Gaborik shook his head, and she sighed.

'Hey!' Pani shouted suddenly. 'I've lost my necklace! It must have fallen off in the snow somewhere!'

'Oh, no,' Mandy said, immediately looking around for some sign of it. Nanook decided she would join in, snuffling around Mandy's legs as she crouched over to study the churned-up snow all about her. Gaborik jogged over to help too, covering the snowy distance between them in a few large strides.

'Is it the same one you were wearing yesterday?' Mandy asked.

'Yes,' said Pani. 'The silver one with apatite . . .'

Mandy stood up, as straight as an arrow. 'What did you say?'

Pani looked at her, puzzled. 'I just said it's the silver one with—'

'*Apatite!*' Mandy exclaimed. 'You were telling me on the sled about your mum making jewellery from the local stones! Can you get those stones here in the park?'

Gaborik frowned at her. 'Yes, some of the elders used to mine them here. There are many rich seams in the local rock where the crystals grow naturally. But I don't see—'

Mandy's heart was racing with excitement. 'What if Mr Ellison wasn't saying he had an appetite for caribou after all! What if he'd been told there were lots of caribou near one of those seams of *apatite*! Apatite for caribou!'

'Wait,' breathed Gaborik. 'I know of a place . . . quite close to one of the old lapis lazuli mines. The ground is crunchy and pink, it's a seam they never mined . . . and it's not far from a big waterfall where the caribou sometimes shelter in hard weather.'

'Is it near here?' Mandy asked him anxiously.

'A few miles away.' His face clouded. 'And to the north of the valley. Simonie and your father have set off for the south.'

Mandy stared at Pani and Gaborik in horror. 'But if we're right, then they'll never find Mr Ellison! They're going completely the wrong way!'

Seven

For a moment, everyone just stared at each other as the realisation sank in. Then Gaborik pulled out his mobile phone. 'I must call them,' he said, his long fingers stabbing at the numbers.

Mandy bit her lip as they all waited in silence for Simonie to pick up.

'It's no good,' Gaborik said finally. 'His phone isn't switched on.'

'It was playing up when he was trying to

call Thomas Tupilak, remember?' said Mandy. 'What if it's gone completely dead?'

Pani groaned. 'We'll never get through to them!'

'Perhaps he's only turned it off for now to save power,' Gaborik suggested. 'We'll keep trying. Meanwhile, I'll try your mother, Pani. Simonie might phone her later, and she can pass on what we think has happened.'

'But she won't be in!' Pani realised. 'This is her day for selling jewellery!'

'My mum might be there,' said Mandy. 'Dad might phone in to talk to her. It's worth a try!'

But the Nanogaks' phone only rang and rang.

'I suppose Mum might be sleeping because of her cold,' Mandy said glumly.

'So what are we going to do?' Pani said urgently. 'Those poor caribou . . . Mr Ellison and Mr Page could be shooting at them as we speak!'

Mandy nodded worriedly. 'Please, Gaborik, can't we go to this apatite place ourselves to try and stop them?'

'I don't know, Mandy,' Gaborik said, frowning. 'Simonie told us to stay here.'

'That's because he thought *he* was going to stop Mr Ellison,' Mandy protested. 'But if he's going the wrong way . . .'

Gaborik sighed. 'We don't know for sure that's true . . .'

'Can't we just go there and check?' Pani begged. 'If we're wrong there's no harm done, is there?'

'Please!' Mandy added.

Gaborik looked at their anxious faces and shook his head wearily. 'I can see I'll get no rest from either of you until we've had a look.'

'Yes!' Mandy punched the air. Pani flung her arms around her. At last they would be doing something that might help the caribou.

Suddenly Nanook reared up on her hind legs, leaning her front paws against Pani's chest and looking up at her. Her tail was wagging in a tight circle.

'There's something in her mouth,' said Mandy, as something pink and sparkling caught the light.

'It's my necklace!' Pani gasped, unhooking the flimsy silver chain from the husky's teeth

and fussing her under her chin. 'Well done, Nanook! Clever girl!'

'Solomon would call that a good omen,' Gaborik decided. 'What is lost shall be found.'

It took them less than an hour to prepare the other sled and harness up the dogs for the trip. Gaborik kept trying Simonie's mobile phone but each time there was no answer, and each time the look on his face grew more troubled.

Mandy knew Gaborik was unhappy about leaving the tourists alone. They were already frustrated at the long delay to their trip. In the end Gaborik called everyone in the lodge together and explained what he was planning to do. Luckily, they all understood the importance of protecting the caribou and finding the missing members of their party. No one argued against him.

'The sooner we find Mr Ellison and Mr

Page, the sooner the trip can get going again,' Gaborik reminded them. 'I will be taking the two girls with me to the apatite seam near the old mine. I ask the rest of you not to wander far from the lodge.' He turned to Mr Richards. 'While I'm gone, I'd like you to look after things here. Is that all right?'

Mr Richards looked around at the others and nodded. 'If everyone else agrees, I'd be happy to.'

The group murmured their approval. Everyone seemed much friendlier by the time Gaborik had finished speaking. It was obvious that the tourists respected his determination to safeguard the wildlife of the National Park. Now Mr Richards and the others were watching from the lodge windows as Gaborik made the final checks on the sled and stepped on to the driving platform at the back.

As Gaborik ordered the dogs away and the sled started moving, a cheer went up from the lodge. Mandy and Pani gave each other nervous smiles, and settled down for a very different journey – not a pleasant trip into the countryside, but an urgent rescue mission where every second counted.

After about an hour the landscape began to change. The rolling snowy hills began to level out, and they found themselves on a vast icy plain that stretched out into the distance. Occasionally the sled hissed past massive boulders, lying around like grey haystacks in a giant's field.

'Where did they come from?' Mandy wondered aloud. 'They look like they just fell out of the sky!'

'Thousands of years ago a great glacier covered this land,' Gaborik explained. 'A moving wall of ice that scraped along the ground. It carried rocks like this along with it. When the glacier melted, it just dropped them here.' He looked round and smiled.

'We allow that kind of littering in the park!'

His words reminded Mandy of the picnic site they'd found yesterday. The more she thought about it, the less she could understand how any tourist could leave their rubbish behind in this beautiful park.

They journeyed on in silence. Gaborik was concentrating on driving the sled, and Mandy and Pani were feeling too anxious to chat. The only sound was the creaking of the sled, the hissing of its runners as they scraped over the snow and the tireless footfalls of the huskies as they pushed on without protest.

The wind numbed Mandy's face and made her eyes water. She wiped them dry with her fleecy red scarf and huddled down even further inside the furry hood of her warm parka.

'Look there, Mandy!' Pani shouted

suddenly, pointing behind them. 'Behind the boulder. Caribou!'

Mandy craned her neck to see. At first she thought she was looking at the branches of a tree growing behind the stone. Then she saw it was the antlers of a large caribou, peering at the sled. Its deer-like head was cocked to one side, as if it were listening to them.

'It's huge,' Mandy breathed. 'I've seen a woodland caribou but they're much smaller.' She remembered the caribou in Labrador that had collided with her dad's truck and been taken to a local wildlife centre for treatment. The sight of the majestic animal in front of her made Mandy even more determined that no harm should come to any caribou if she could possibly help it.

'Do you think we're getting close?' Pani called back to Gaborik.

'I reckon the old mine is that way,' he answered, pointing to the left. 'And the fissure of apatite should be close by. But I can't be sure about any of this. It's a long time since I was last travelling this way.'

'You'll get us there,' Mandy said quietly. 'I know it.'

The sled seemed to bump along even faster, as if the huskies themselves sensed the importance of their mission. The seat of the sled was hard beneath Mandy, and her bones were starting to ache from the constant rattling at high speed over the frozen land. Ahead of them the land sloped upwards to a snowy crest, but the dogs kept on with no sign of slowing. If she closed her eyes Mandy could almost imagine she was on some incredible fairground ride.

Gaborik instructed the huskies to stop when they reached the top. 'We've made good progress so far,' he said. 'And it's past lunchtime. Let's stop and eat.'

Mandy nodded, and she and Pani unwrapped the sandwiches they had brought for the journey. They munched together in silence.

From the hilltop they could see for miles around. Mandy felt as if they were as high as the winter sun, which was edging round to the west, low in the white sky. The sub-Arctic wastes stretched around them, crisp and sparkling, with nothing to distract the eye except for the occasional boulder or a patch of scrubby vegetation. But at the line of the horizon, where sky and snow seemed to meet and mingle, there was a patch of dusky pink. Was it just the first stirrings of sunset or . . .

'Gaborik, could that be it?' Mandy asked urgently, pointing to the pink patch in the distance.

He nodded slowly. 'It could just be.' He called to the dogs.

Mandy felt the sled pick up speed as it bounced and slithered downhill. 'Hold on, caribou,' she whispered. 'We're coming!'

* * *

'That's it all right,' said Gaborik as they approached closer to the stretch of glittering red-hued rock. 'We've found the apatite. Now we just need to see if Ellison and Page are here.'

The site of the apatite seam was extraordinary. It looked like a huge skip had just emptied out the sparkling stones over the whole area.

'There's enough to make a thousand necklaces, Pani,' Mandy remarked in wonder. 'How come no one's taken it all?'

'Apatite is not really a gemstone,' Gaborik told her, peering ahead for any sign that the missing men had passed this way. 'It's just a mineral, mainly used for making fertilisers.'

Pani looked a little crestfallen at this, so Mandy nudged her and smiled. 'Prettiest fertiliser I've ever seen!'

The sled crunched and scraped onwards over the rough ground. Just around the corner they found something that definitely didn't belong in this landscape. A green two-man tent had been pitched in the snow, the canvas billowing about as the wind tugged at it.

'A camp!' Pani declared.

'Newly pitched too,' said Gaborik as he slowed the sled. 'No snow on it . . . it must be theirs. Looks like you were right about them coming here, Mandy.' He called the men's names but there was no sign of them. 'Where have those idiots gone?' he muttered. 'It'll be dark soon.'

Mandy shivered. Looking around for another clue, she noticed a curious zigzag trail of markings in the snow behind them. 'Which animal made these?' she asked.

'Foxes?' Pani suggested.

'Or *amaqqut*,' Gaborik said grimly.

Mandy looked at him, waiting for a translation.

'Wolves. Perhaps we're not the only ones looking for our friends. The wolves might have smelled their food, and be after an early snack. Come on. We must hurry.'

He urged the huskies on again, but the ground was so puckered and rocky round the apatite seam they could only make slow progress.

'Let's go on foot,' Gaborik suggested. 'We don't want to risk damaging the sled. Just stay close to me, all right?'

Pani and Mandy both nodded, and helped Gaborik unclip the dogs' harnesses so they could go on their leads.

'Nanook's such a brilliant dog,' Mandy said, fixing the lead in place. 'Perhaps she'll make a good bloodhound too, and lead us straight to them!' Nanook looked up at her steadily, as if she understood what was happening.

The dogs jostled each other as they surged forwards over the rocky ground, tugging against their leads. Gaborik had hold of four of the dogs, while Pani held on to Nanook and Mandy walked Okpik. The little dog kept sniffing the ground as if picking up a strong trail, and Mandy had to pause several times to wait for him.

'What's wrong, boy?' she asked as Okpik started to whine softly. She patted his solid flank. 'We really have to keep moving, you know. We're close now, I'm sure we are . . .'

Suddenly a chilling, baying call sounded from close by. To Mandy it seemed much louder and more frightening than when she'd heard it at the site of the abandoned picnic.

'Wolves,' said Pani as another howl went up. She looked very pale. Even though wolves didn't normally attack people, it made sense to keep a good distance from them, especially with the dogs around.

All the dogs seemed to erupt as one into a wild frenzy of barking – all except Nanook. She strained forward, apparently unafraid, struggling to see what lay over the brow of the hill ahead of them.

'Follow me,' Gaborik instructed them, hurrying up the rise. 'It's all right, I've got the flare gun. If the wolves do cause us any problems we can scare them away.' He muttered soothing words to the huskies skittering about his legs.

Mandy scrambled after him. Suddenly, she saw a strange figure looming up before them at the top of the slope, a dark silhouette against the sky. She skidded to a halt, shock making her breath catch in her throat.

The figure was carrying a spear in one of its huge hands.

'It's the Tuniit!' gasped Pani beside her, her face white with fear. 'The stories were true! The Tuniit are angry that the animals are being hunted!'

Eight

'Don't be afraid,' Gaborik told them quickly. 'It's just one of the *innuksuk* I told you about, a stone carving. It's one of the ancient marking posts. It can guide us.'

Mandy let out her breath in a long sigh of relief.

Pani smiled sheepishly. 'Sorry, Mandy, I didn't mean to scare you. When I saw it I just thought—'

Nanook interrupted her with a loud bark.

She was still straining to see beyond the rise, her pointed ears twitching.

As they scrambled closer to the top, Mandy could see that the figure was carved quite crudely from rock, like a human-shaped pillar. 'Why did the Inuit make it in the shape of a man?' she asked.

'Believe it or not, to help them hunt caribou,' Gaborik said, peering around the

darkening landscape. 'The animals would see what looked like a hunter, and run the other way – towards where the *real* Inuit were lying in wait for them.'

He was interrupted by another high-pitched howl. The sound seemed to be coming from all around them. Okpik started barking again, furiously. Nanook pulled hard against Pani's grip on her lead, her eyes gleaming. She sniffed the air as if trying to catch a scent. Then, as the howling faded away, a sound like an explosion went off nearby, rumbling like thunder.

'That was a gun!' Mandy gasped. Beside her, Okpik flinched and whined. But Nanook seemed to take no notice of the sinister noise. She leaped forwards at the sound of the shot, yanking her lead right out of Pani's hand. Then she sped down the snowy slope and vanished behind a large rock.

'Nanook, come back!' shouted Pani. 'I

couldn't stop her!' she cried miserably to Gaborik.

'After her, quick!' said Gaborik. He set off at a run, the other huskies bounding in front of him, their ears flat with alarm.

Mandy slipped and slid in the snow behind Gaborik as she raced to keep up. 'It's all right,' she said over and over again, realising she was trying to convince herself as much as the terrified huskies.

A high-pitched yelp sounded somewhere ahead of them. 'Nanook,' Pani breathed, fearing the worst as they rounded the rock to where her dog had last been seen.

Ahead of them was a shallow gully. Huddled together to their right were Tom Ellison and Ben Page. The men looked terrified. One rifle lay discarded on the icy ground, but Mr Ellison was pointing his in the air. The wisps of smoke coming from the barrel showed that he had fired the shot they had heard.

Mandy followed their horrified gaze and stopped dead in her tracks. Just a few metres away from them was a huge wolf. From the tracks in the churned-up snow, there had clearly been many more here. Perhaps the others had been frightened away by the gunshot. But this wolf remained, snarling, its tongue flicking over its sharp, pointed teeth, as it glared at the two men.

Mandy's heart sank when she saw that Nanook was standing between the wolf and the men. The husky was staring at the wolf curiously with her wide pale eyes. Unlike the other huskies, her fur lay flat along her back, and she didn't seem scared at all.

'Everybody keep very, very still,' Gaborik commanded in a low, clear voice. 'If the wolf thinks you're going to attack, it might try to get you first!' One of the huskies he was holding was Sedna. She began to growl threateningly, and he shushed her.

'Oh, please come away, Nanook!' Pani sounded close to tears. 'Please, girl!'

'I've got a flare gun in my pocket,' Gaborik told them. 'I'll fire it in the air and scare the wolf away.'

'But you might scare Nanook away too!' Pani cried.

Mandy gazed helplessly at Nanook and the wolf. While Nanook was sleek and muscled, the wolf was lean and hungry-looking, with matted, unkempt fur that was dirty white with distinctive charcoal-coloured smears. Its eyes were cold and yellow, narrowed at Nanook and the two men. It bared its teeth and started to growl.

'I'll show the wretched thing,' muttered Mr Ellison. He lowered his gun and squinted along the barrel.

'No!' Mandy cried. She saw the wolf tense itself, ready to spring.

Gaborik raised his hand to gesture at Mr Ellison not to fire. But at the same moment,

Sedna tore her lead free of his grip and sprinted bravely forward.

Before it could turn, the wolf tumbled backwards under the husky's fierce attack. The two creatures snapped at each other, kicking up flurries of thick snow.

To Mandy's horror, she saw that Mr Ellison was still preparing to shoot. 'Stop! You could hit Sedna!' she yelled.

Gaborik thrust the leads of the remaining dogs into Mandy's shaking hands and ran towards the two men. Mr Ellison looked up in surprise to find the burly Inuit man bearing down on him. A moment later, he and Ben Page went down in a heap as Gaborik cannoned into them. The rifle spun through the air. To Mandy's relief, it landed in the snow without going off.

But Sedna and the wolf were still fighting.

'Back, Sedna!' Mandy shouted. 'You've scared it enough, let it go!'

Sedna showed no signs of having heard.

Her jaws were clamped on the wolf's back. It kept twisting its head and snapping back at her but it couldn't reach. Every time it tried to twist free it only managed to drive Sedna's teeth further into its skin.

Then Nanook charged into the fray.

'Not you too, Nanook!' cried Pani in despair. 'Come back! Leave the wolf alone!'

But it wasn't the wolf Nanook was lunging for, teeth bared. It was Sedna. With an angry howl Nanook launched herself at the other husky, biting at one of Sedna's hind legs. The bigger dog let go of the wolf, confused to find herself coming under attack. The wolf stumbled clear, lurching towards Mandy and Pani and the rest of the dogs.

'Keep away!' Mandy shouted, yanking the dogs closer to her.

The wolf stared at her for a moment, before shaking its massive head as if clearing its senses. Then it turned and pounded away, vanishing into the dusk.

Meanwhile, Sedna was snarling with rage, her jaws scissoring at Nanook's muscular flank, teeth tearing at her fur.

'Stop!' Pani yelled. 'Stop fighting, you two!'

Gaborik waded in between the two fighting dogs, trying to separate them. Without thinking, Mandy shoved the dog leads into Pani's hands. Then she skidded down into the gully, her only thought to pull the two dogs apart.

'Keep back, Mandy, it's dangerous!' Gaborik said through gritted teeth.

But Mandy had seen Nanook's terrified eyes as the husky realised she'd picked a fight she couldn't win. Mandy held out her arms to Nanook, trying to draw her away by her collar, but her gloves made her clumsy. She pulled them off and slipped freezing fingers down between the cold leather strap and hot, wet fur. She felt Sedna's teeth scrape against her arm, and was grateful she had the thick padding of her parka for protection.

At last, Gaborik had a proper hold on Sedna, and pulled her away. He looked up at Mandy and his eyes flashed with anger. 'You stupid girl,' he said to her as he stroked and soothed the frantic Sedna. 'You could've got yourself badly hurt!'

Mandy looked at him in surprise, blinking away the tears of fear and relief that were threatening to come. Nanook was whining softly, her head in Mandy's lap. 'But ... I couldn't just stand here and let them hurt each other ...'

Gaborik's angry face softened. 'Apparently not.'

Pani came over with the crowd of dogs and threw her arms around Mandy. She was shaking all over. 'You were so brave, Mandy, but you shouldn't have done that.'

Mandy hugged her back, then took a deep, shaky breath. Okpik pushed forward to Nanook, sniffing her anxiously. She was breathing deeply and quickly, her eyes only half-open, her ears flattened against her head.

'It's all right, girl,' Mandy told the husky. 'It's all over now.'

'Is she hurt?' Gaborik asked.

'I – I'm not sure,' Mandy said. 'I think she could be in shock.'

'Why would she attack Sedna like that?' Pani wondered, gazing down at Nanook with worried eyes. 'It looked as if she was trying to protect the wolf!'

'I don't know what she was doing,' Gaborik admitted. He whistled through his teeth. 'Just don't scare me like that again, old girl!' Then he swung round to face Tom Ellison and Ben Page, who were painfully picking themselves up from the icy ground. 'And that goes double for you two idiots!'

Ben Page shook his head in amazement. 'Those wolves . . . they found us so quickly!'

'A wolf can hear a watch ticking at ten metres,' Gaborik said sourly. 'I expect they could hear the noise you were making pitching your camp miles away.'

Tom Ellison grimaced and pulled a small parcel from his coat pocket. 'And I guess they could smell these roast chicken sandwiches, right?'

Gaborik nodded. 'Right.'

Ben Page sighed. 'I suppose it was Tupilak who told you where to find us?'

'No,' Gaborik said, 'it was Mandy, actually.'

It was the first time Mandy had seen Mr Ellison entirely lost for words.

'And lucky for you she worked it out,' Gaborik continued. 'You've put your lives in danger, wasted my time and spoilt the entire trip.'

'All right.' Mr Ellison held up his hands in a 'back off' gesture. 'All right, we're sorry. I guess we didn't think it was that big a deal. Tupilak told us he'd square it with you guys.'

'Yeah,' added Ben Page, 'he said he often took people out this way from the main party. He said he'd pick us up later, and that we'd join up with you again tonight.'

Gaborik shook his head. 'He didn't tell any of us anything.'

Ben Page turned crossly to Mr Ellison. 'I told you he was no good. Like the way he reckoned he had to take us here in the dead of night because the hunting was best in the early morning.'

'You've not . . . shot anything, have you?' Mandy asked in a small voice.

'Not a thing,' sighed Mr Ellison. 'All day. Reckon those wolves spooked the caribou clear to the other side of the park.'

'Oh, thank goodness!' Mandy looked up at Pani with a broad grin, and felt a knot untie itself in her stomach. 'We got here in time!'

Pani nodded excitedly. 'Now we can get out of here and head for home! How is Nanook doing, Mandy?'

'I'm not sure,' Mandy said honestly. The

husky's head was still in her lap. Her eyes were closed now, and she was starting to shiver. Her breathing was irregular, little clouds of steam bursting from her dry nose. 'Wake up, Nanook,' Mandy whispered, stroking the dog's ear with her gloved hand. 'Don't go to sleep now.'

'We should try to get back to the sled,' Gaborik suggested.

Mandy carefully pulled out her hand from under Nanook's collar. With the temperature dropping as darkness fell, she'd lost all feeling in her fingers. She held them up to blow on them – then gasped.

They were sticky with blood.

'Oh, Nanook!' she cried. 'Gaborik, Pani, she's bleeding!'

'Where?' Gaborik asked urgently, coming to see.

Mandy tried to keep calm, pulling off her other glove and undoing Nanook's collar. 'She has a gash on her neck, it looks quite deep,' she said. 'I'll try to put some pressure on it to stop the bleeding.' Then she started feeling round the husky's trembling body. Nanook whined as Mandy's fingers pressed against the left side of her chest. 'Heartbeat's still quite strong . . . but she's hurt her side . . .' A lump seemed to form in Mandy's throat as she went on checking, making it hard to go on talking. 'And one of her legs is giving her pain.' Mandy bit her lip, trying to keep calm. 'I could be missing something serious, I'm not an expert. Oh, if only Mum and Dad were here!'

'Sedna, how could you!' Pani yelled, helpless with fear and anger.

'Pani, she didn't start the fight,' Gaborik pointed out gently.

'We need a vet,' Pani went on, her voice trembling. 'Quickly.'

'Where will we find one out here?' Tom Ellison enquired, sounding anxious.

Mandy realised he was right. They were

all alone in a freezing wilderness, the only people for miles and miles around. Where could help possibly come from?

Mandy untucked her scarf from her parka and pulled it off. Then she wrapped it carefully round Nanook. 'We must try to keep her warm.'

Pani was already pulling off her own scarf. Soon Nanook was swaddled in the makeshift blanket. Her pointed black nose poked out from beneath the bright red and yellow fleecy material.

'So when is Tupilak coming for you two?' Gaborik asked, turning to Mr Ellison and Ben Page. 'I mean, even he wouldn't be dumb enough to leave you all alone here. So he must be close by. Perhaps he'll help.'

'He was supposed to call to arrange a time for pick-up,' said Ben Page. 'But he hasn't.'

'If Simonie's phone isn't working, there's only one way we can get a vet's help all the way out here,' Mandy said slowly.

Gaborik reached for his mobile phone. 'Your mother.'

'But no one's been answering at home!' Pani pointed out.

'Let's try again,' said Mandy. 'Maybe someone will answer this time. Dial your house, Pani!'

Pani struggled a bit with the phone, as she was still holding on to four of the huskies. Kilabuk, Mikijuk and Nunatta were sitting obediently at her feet, but Okpik was nervously pawing at her leg. Pani crouched down to give him some attention while she listened to the ringing tone. Then her mouth opened wide in a surprised smile. 'Someone's answered! It's your mum, Mandy!'

Mandy's heart jumped in her chest and she felt a wave of relief flood through her.

'Mrs Hope, it's Pani.' Mandy could see her friend was struggling to stay calm but her voice was still shaking. 'We need your help.

I'm – I'm going to pass you over to Mandy.'

Mandy took the phone from her. 'Mum!' she yelled into the mouthpiece.

'Mandy, are you all right? What's going on?' came Mrs Hope's voice, thick with cold.

'It's Nanook, Mum . . .' As quickly and clearly as she could, Mandy told her mum all that had happened.

Mrs Hope was clearly shocked. 'Goodness, Mandy . . . I can't understand how . . . Look, are *you* all right?'

'I'm fine, Mum, but we have to help Nanook!'

Instantly, Mrs Hope's tone became calm and professional. 'OK, Mandy,' she began, 'where's Nanook now?'

'Lying on her side with her head in my lap,' Mandy told her. 'We've covered her in scarves.'

'That's good,' said Mrs Hope. 'It's vital she's kept warm. Her body temperature will have dropped anyway with the shock of the fight. But make sure she's not wrapped up too tightly, you could be putting more pressure on a fracture.'

Mandy just hoped she could carry out her mum's instructions over the long distance. She'd cared for injured dogs before, but never in conditions as extreme as these. She pulled at the scarves a little. She didn't think they were too tight but she didn't want to take any chances.

'Now, it'll be dangerous to move her, but I don't see you've got much choice.' Mrs Hope didn't mince her words. 'If she doesn't reach shelter, she could die. Can you get back to the lodge?'

'It's miles away!' Mandy told her.

'The mine,' Gaborik put in, stroking Sedna's back with a firm hand. 'There will be shelter at the lapis lazuli mine. That's where we must head for.'

Mandy told her mum, who agreed it seemed the only option.

'But how can we get her there?' Pani asked, wiping her eyes.

'We could make a kind of hammock from the scarves,' Gaborik suggested.

Mandy passed on the idea to her mum, but Mrs Hope rejected it. 'Too soft,' she said. 'There'll be no support, the poor thing will be swinging about all over the place. If she's got internal injuries, they could be made far worse.'

'Could we fetch the sled?' said Pani. 'Take her back on that?'

Gaborik shook his head. 'The sled doesn't travel well over the rocky ground, remember?'

'Oh, if only we had a proper stretcher of some kind,' Mandy said, feeling utterly helpless.

'Well, we haven't,' said Ben Page sourly.

'But we *could* have!' said Mr Ellison.

Everyone turned to look at him.

'OK,' he said, clapping his hands together

briskly. 'Ben, go back to our tent and get one of the sleeping bags from the holdall.' His friend looked at him strangely. 'Move it, Ben!'

'A sleeping bag won't do,' Mandy told him. 'It would be good for keeping her warm, but it's too soft to carry her in. It won't give Nanook any support.'

'Exactly,' Tom Ellison told her. 'It needs a framework to make it a proper stretcher. Two poles either side to keep the fabric taut. Right?' He stooped down and picked up Ben Page's discarded rifle, and waved his own. 'Here are your two poles!'

'That's . . .' Mandy felt a glimmer of hope. 'That's a brilliant idea, Mr Ellison!'

The Canadian shrugged.

'All right, Mandy,' said Mrs Hope over the phone. 'While that gets sorted out, can you tell me exactly where this mine is? I just heard Mary coming back in. We can come out to you in the truck.'

'Gaborik must know the way,' Mandy said. 'He told the other tourists back at the lodge where he was going, in case Dad and Simonie came back. I'll put him on.'

'Hi, Emily,' Gaborik said to Mrs Hope. 'Am I glad to be talking to you!' As he gave her rough directions to the mine, Ben Page returned with the sleeping bag.

'Turn it inside out,' Mr Ellison instructed. 'The lining will be warmer for her to lie on.' He tossed Ben Page his unloaded rifle. 'Now, push this down one side. I'll do the same here.' With that done, the two men took hold of each end of their rifles and lifted the sleeping bag.

Gaborik had finished giving the directions. He passed the phone back to Mandy and inspected the makeshift stretcher. 'If you can keep the material at full stretch, I think it will work,' he said.

'Mum,' said Mandy, swallowing hard. 'We're going to try and move her.'

'All right, Mandy, good luck. I'm going to organise the cavalry at this end, OK?'

'OK, Mum,' Mandy said. 'See you soon.'

'See you *very* soon. Bye, love.'

Mandy disconnected, and took a deep, shaky breath. Darkness had fallen as, quite suddenly, the sky had turned black, flecked with tiny yellow stars. By the light of the cold crescent moon, Mandy helped Gaborik gently shift Nanook on to the cosy lining of the sleeping bag, making sure her head, back and pelvis were supported. Then Mr Ellison and Mr Page lifted the home-made stretcher.

'Let's go,' said Gaborik, four eager dogs straining at the leads in his hands.

They had already travelled a long way, but Mandy knew the most difficult and dangerous stage of the journey was just beginning.

Nine

They walked back the way they had come, the snow crunching endlessly under their feet. It was dark and difficult to see anything. From time to time Gaborik paused and looked keenly around for anything familiar that might guide their way. It was taking him time to get his bearings in this unfamiliar part of the park – and time was just what Nanook didn't have unless they could reach shelter soon.

Pani broke the heavy silence with an excited shout. 'Up there, look!' She pointed ahead of them. 'The *innuksuk*!'

Sure enough, there was the dark figure with his spear high on the hillside, his thin silhouette blocking out a scattering of stars. The icy air turned Mandy's sigh of relief into a cloud of steam. 'It's not far from there to the sled,' she told the two men carrying Nanook. 'But it's quite a steep slope.'

'We'll be careful with her,' Mr Ellison assured her. Mandy was surprised to see this gentler side to the Canadian. But then, anyone could see that Nanook was a very special dog. And why had she attacked Sedna and not the wolf? It just didn't make sense . . .

Carefully they climbed the slope, and Gaborik studied the marking stone. Strange symbols had been carved into the rock. 'Inuit directions,' he murmured. 'I was right. The old mine is to the west of this apatite seam. Let's get going!'

Once the scramble down the slope was over, they put Nanook on her stretcher in the back of the sled while Gaborik harnessed the other huskies. Soon they were under way. Pani and Mandy sat on either side of Nanook, supporting her head and trying to keep her warm.

Mandy slipped her hand inside the sleeping bag to feel the pulse on the inside of Nanook's hind leg. The beat was weak and erratic. She bit her lip. 'Stay with us, Nanook,' she whispered. 'Please, girl, stay with us!'

The dog-sled made good speed over the ice, even with only five huskies running instead of six, but Mandy felt as if the journey was taking for ever. Finally, the dark shape of a building came into sight.

'It must be the prospectors' *qammaq*,' Gaborik said, turning to Mandy and Pani with a look of triumph. 'Their hut! We've made it!'

The dogs pulled up in front of a gated fence. Mr Ellison leaped out and opened the gate, which creaked noisily open on ancient hinges. Gaborik ordered the dogs to run on straight away. Mr Ellison followed them along the frozen track on foot.

'Right,' said Gaborik, as they pulled up outside the large, rickety-looking hut. 'Let's get her inside.'

Ben Page helped Mandy lift the stretcher, while Gaborik took a lantern from the sled and lit their way to the door of the hut.

'Won't it be locked?' Pani asked fearfully.

'I'll force it open if I have to,' Gaborik said grimly. But after a couple of firm shoves, the stiff door creaked open. Gaborik led them inside, holding the lantern before him and peering into the dark corners of the room.

'Just checking nothing got in before us,' he explained. Then he brought the lantern over to a table beside a grimy window. 'This looks like our best bet for a hospital bed,' he said.

Pani cleared away some boxes of files and pieces of paper, and then Mandy and Ben Page gently laid Nanook's stretcher down on the table. 'All right, girl,' Mandy told the dog in what she hoped was a reassuring voice. 'The travelling's over. You can rest now. Rest and get well.'

The husky whimpered softly to herself. Mandy stroked the dog's head.

Suddenly the door swung open behind them. Everyone jumped, but it was only Tom Ellison. He looked soberly at Nanook. 'Hope she'll be OK. Anything I can do to help?'

'Actually, there is,' Gaborik told him. 'You can help me bed down the rest of the dogs. We'll look around, see if we can find an outhouse or something, somewhere to shelter them until help arrives.' He turned to Mandy. 'Will you two be all right here with Nanook?'

'Of course!' Pani told him. 'I think she needs some water, though.'

'Yes, that's a good idea,' said Mandy. 'We can bathe her cut too. It's still bleeding a bit.'

'I'll fetch you some of our drinking water,' said Tom Ellison. He turned and left the hut.

'It's a shame we don't have some kind of bandage,' said Gaborik. 'The first aid kit's on your father's sled.'

'Maybe I could make one out of my shirt sleeve,' Mandy suggested.

'Here, allow me,' Ben Page said. He shrugged off his coat and produced a hunting knife from his trouser pocket. Then he started cutting into his own shirt sleeve. When he'd finished he handed over the improvised bandage to Mandy. A moment later, Tom Ellison reappeared with a water bottle and a dog dish.

Mandy smiled gratefully. 'Thanks.'

'We'll take care of the others,' said

Gaborik. He walked over to the door, and ushered the other men through. 'Back soon.'

Once they'd bathed the cut on her neck, Pani poured some water into Nanook's bowl. Mandy placed it beside the dog. However, it was clear that she was far too weak to be able to stand and drink from it.

'We need something shallower,' Mandy decided. 'Something she can lap from while she's lying down. Let's look around, see if we can find a saucer or a plate or something.'

Gingerly they explored the ramshackle cabin. In one corner, Mandy found a cardboard box.

'What's inside it?' asked Pani.

Mandy reached in and pulled out a tin. 'Cans of food,' she said. 'This one's minced beef, I think.'

Pani screwed up her nose. 'Ugh! How long has that been lying around for?'

Mandy tossed her the tin and kept on looking.

'Wait a minute,' said Pani. 'This tin is new. It's not dusty or anything. It was bought from Little Tulung's grocery store in Kimmirut, I recognise the price label.' She frowned. 'He's only been open six months.'

'Gaborik said the mine had been abandoned for years,' Mandy said, puzzled.

'But this place wasn't locked up, was it?' Pani reminded her.

'Hey, I've found some plates,' said Mandy. 'A tin opener too, and some knives and forks.' She looked over at Pani, suddenly uneasy. 'They all look clean and new as well.'

'And the table,' Pani realised, crossing back over to check on Nanook. 'When I cleared all those files off it . . . there was hardly any dust on them. They should all be covered in dirt.'

'You know what I think?' asked Mandy, pouring some of the water on to the plate. 'Someone's been here before us. They're using this place as a kind of base.'

She pushed the plate right up to Nanook's hot, dry nose, but the husky showed no interest. Mandy wasn't going to give up that easily. She dipped her finger in the cold liquid and held it to Nanook's mouth, dabbing it on her tongue. 'Come on, girl. Just a sip . . .' She splashed a little more over the dog's jaws. Slowly, Nanook flicked her tongue over Mandy's fingers. 'That's right!' Mandy whispered. She dipped her fingers in again, and Nanook licked at them with a little more enthusiasm.

Pani looked around and turned up her nose. 'It's horrible here. Who would come all the way out here just to sit in this place?' she asked.

'If someone came this way often,' said Mandy slowly, 'it wouldn't *be* out of the way, would it?'

Pani's eyes widened. 'You mean Tupilak?'

Mandy nodded. 'That's right.'

'But his office is in Kimmirut. It's really

big, in the centre of town. Why would he keep things here? Unless . . .' A thought seemed to strike the Inuit girl, and suddenly she began scooping up the files she had cleared away.

Mandy finished her sentence for her. 'Unless they're things he doesn't want anyone to know about!'

Pani opened the first file and started leafing through the paperwork inside. 'These contracts belong to the *tiriaq* all right.'

'Contracts for what?' Mandy asked, curious.

Pani looked up at her, her dark eyes very serious. 'Now we know why he keeps this stuff here,' she said. 'Look!'

Still keeping one wet hand by Nanook's mouth, Mandy took one of the contracts. 'It's mostly in Inuit writing, I can't read it,' she said. Then she spotted something. 'Hey, this signature – it's Tom Ellison's!'

'The contract says he has to pay Tupilak for taking him hunting, and a further payment for every animal they hunt on the trip,' Pani told her. 'There are loads more like it in here. Tupilak's been running an illegal hunting business, right in the heart of the park! Dad always thought he was up to something like this, but he never had the proof to get him caught.'

'Because it's all kept in here!' Mandy breathed.

Pani looked at her, her eyes shining. 'There's all the evidence here Dad needs to get him stopped!'

They heard the door open behind them. 'Didn't take you long to bed down the dogs,' Mandy called without looking round.

But it was an unexpected voice that answered her, low and threatening. 'What are you two doing here?'

Mandy's stomach lurched with fear. She had heard that voice before, back at the dog-sled race in Kimmirut. She turned slowly. Pani was staring in horror at the weasley figure in the doorway.

'This is my property,' said Thomas Tupilak coldly. 'And you are trespassing.' He stepped inside and closed the door of the hut behind him.

Ten

Mandy glanced at Pani, who was hurriedly trying to put Thomas Tupilak's papers away.

But it was too late. The *tiriaq*'s thin face darkened as he saw what they had found. 'How dare you?' he hissed. 'Those are my private papers. Leave those files where they are.'

'I'm ... I'm sorry, Mr Tupilak,' Pani mumbled. Mandy could tell she was terrified. She crammed more of the paperwork back into the folder. 'I knocked the file over, and they . . . they just fell out.'

'You are lying,' growled Thomas Tupilak. 'You are spying on me. How did you find this place? Did your father bring you here?'

'No!' Mandy protested. 'We were just looking for shelter! Look!' She pointed to Nanook. The husky was fast asleep, snuggled into the sleeping bag on the tabletop,

breathing more regularly at last. 'Nanook got into a fight—'

Tupilak didn't even glance at the table. 'I do not care about your stupid excuses,' he said in a harsh voice.

'Excuses!' Mandy couldn't believe what she was hearing. 'If you hadn't taken Mr Ellison off hunting, we wouldn't have had to come looking for him, and the wolves would never have come, and poor Nanook wouldn't be hurt!'

'Those idiot tourists,' said Tupilak dismissively. 'I have just wasted my time going to pick them up at the gully.'

'Mr Ellison and his friend are here,' Pani said quickly. 'They're right outside, with Gaborik.'

'Why, Pani, you sound as though you're afraid of me,' Tupilak said with a smile that revealed his crooked teeth. 'But you have nothing to fear. Not if you are sensible.'

Mandy reached for Pani's hand and gave

it a reassuring squeeze. She felt like her legs were turning to jelly as she took a step back.

Tupilak chuckled. Reaching the table, he stroked Nanook's head softly. 'I see your dog *is* unwell,' he said. Then he smiled. 'I could help her. Take her back to Kimmirut for you and make sure she is looked after.'

'Oh, yes please,' Mandy said desperately. 'She needs a vet, as quickly as possible.'

'So I see. But it would be such a shame if I was *unable* to take her,' Tupilak went on with a cruel grin. 'Imagine if I had to leave her here in the dark and the cold, because I was concerned you might tell someone what you have found.' But the smile froze on his face as the office door was flung open behind him.

'Dad!' cried Mandy, almost laughing with relief.

Adam Hope was framed in the doorway. His tired eyes narrowed as he took in the scene in front of him. 'Well, well. Mr

Thomas Tupilak,' he said. 'We wondered whose truck that was outside.'

'Oh Dad, I'm so pleased to see you!' Mandy exclaimed.

'Is my dad with you?' Pani added hopefully.

'I'm here, Pani.' Simonie Nanogak followed Mr Hope into the gloomy hut. 'Everything's all right now.'

'You're just in time! Nanook's been hurt,' Mandy said, pushing past the stunned Thomas Tupilak to where the injured husky lay on the table. 'I – I tried to do what I could but—'

'Don't worry, Mandy,' said Mr Hope, giving her a quick hug and then turning to study Nanook. 'You did brilliantly. What happened?'

While Mandy started to explain, Thomas Tupilak recovered his voice at last. 'You are all trespassing on my property,' he snarled. 'You must leave here at once.'

Simonie shook his head. 'You don't own

this mine. You are a trespasser here as much as we are.'

Suddenly, Tupilak lunged forward and made a grab for the incriminating papers that Pani was holding. She clutched them closer to her chest and dodged out of the way, running to her father. 'Dad,' she said breathlessly, pressing the crumpled pieces of paper into his hands. 'It's evidence. Proof he's been taking people hunting in the park.'

Mandy nodded fiercely. 'People like Mr Ellison have been paying him to show them the best places to go shooting.'

Simonie quickly glanced through the papers, then looked straight into Tupilak's eyes. 'You're finished,' he said quietly. 'For years, I have suspected what you were up to, but I could never prove it.' He folded the papers and put them in his coat pocket. 'Now you've proved it for me.'

Tupilak laughed nervously, and held out his hands as if appealing to an old friend.

'Come now, Simonie, don't be hasty. You and me – we can be partners. I'm willing to share the trade. Goodness knows there's enough of it.'

Simonie ignored Tupilak's offered hand and shook his head scornfully. 'There won't be any more,' he said gravely. 'Not if I can help it. No more illegal hunts. I'm going to the police.'

Thomas Tupilak clenched his fists. Then he pushed past Simonie, flung open the door and ran from the hut into the cold night. Mandy breathed a huge sigh of relief and sat down heavily on the box of food.

'Scurrying away like the weasel he is,' Simonie said, shaking his head sadly. 'But running will do him no good.' He patted his coat pocket and embraced Pani warmly. 'Not now.'

Mandy gave a thumbs-up to Pani, who beamed back with delight. Then she turned back to her dad. While Simonie and Tupilak had been talking, Mr Hope had been examining Nanook.

'Is she going to be OK?' Mandy asked anxiously.

'You did a good job with her, Mandy,' Mr Hope murmured. 'If you hadn't been here . . .'

'Oh, it was mostly Mum, really,' Mandy told him, blushing. 'She told me what to do over the phone. But how did *you* find us?'

'We headed back to the lodge when we realised we'd been off on a wild goose chase,' Mr Hope explained. 'Mr Richards told us where you'd all gone.' He smiled. 'That was a good guess about the apatite, Mandy.'

'I should've thought of this place myself,' Simonie added, looking around the dilapidated old hut. 'Solomon worked at this mine when he was young.'

'You say you spoke to your mother?' Adam Hope asked.

Mandy nodded. 'She should be on her way here now with Mary.'

'She'll be bringing medical supplies too, so we can patch up Nanook properly,' said Adam Hope. 'That's good news.'

'It should only take a matter of hours to reach here,' said Simonie.

Mandy swallowed and looked nervously at her father. 'But will that be in time?'

Adam Hope smiled at her, and nodded. 'Yes, I think so. Nanook's going to be poorly for a while, but her condition seems stable. She's bruised her ribs and badly sprained her leg, and I'd like to put some stitches in that cut on her neck, but at least nothing's broken. In the meantime I'll get a bandage from the sled's first aid box.' He suddenly noticed the makeshift stretcher that Nanook was still sprawled on. 'Was this your idea, Mandy?'

'No, it was Mr Ellison's,' said Mandy with a big smile.

'Someone call?' said the Canadian dryly as he pushed open the door of the hut. 'They're just finishing up with the dogs back there, thought I'd get back to shelter . . .' he trailed off as he saw both Simonie and Mr Hope glaring at him. 'So, part one of the cavalry's made it here?' he said with a glance at Mandy.

'We've come a long, long way to find you, Mr Ellison,' Simonie said gravely.

'I know, I know. And that wasn't *all* you found, right?' Mr Ellison waved a hand at Nanook on the table and sighed. 'Look, I feel real bad about all this. I know I've wrecked your whole sled-trip.'

'But you really helped us with Nanook,' said Pani. She turned to her dad. 'And Mr Page helped too.'

Mr Hope nodded. 'Nanook's injuries might have been made worse without this stretcher to support her.'

'I'm glad those guns came in useful for

something,' Mr Ellison said ruefully. 'Is the dog OK?'

'Dad says she'll be fine,' Mandy told him.

Mr Ellison rubbed the back of his hand over his forehead as if wiping his brow in relief, but then he frowned. 'Wait a minute, I thought I heard a truck pull up and clear out again. But since I guess that's your dog-sled outside, who else has come to call?'

'Mr Tupilak,' Pani told him.

'So he finally showed, huh?' growled the Canadian darkly. 'I know we were wrong to take off like we did, but he did promise us that he'd fix things with you, Mr Nanogak. We never thought you'd be put to any trouble.'

'But you admit that you paid Thomas Tupilak to take you hunting?' Simonie asked.

'Yes, I did,' Mr Ellison admitted. 'It was a darn fool thing to do as it turned out, but yes, I paid him.'

'And would you be prepared to confirm

this to the police?' Simonie asked. 'With your testimony and the evidence we've found here, we can finish Tupilak for good.'

'If it'll help me and Ben put things right, then sure,' said Mr Ellison. Then he turned to Mr Hope. 'But you know, I reckon there's a few more dogs out there that could do with you giving them the once over while we're waiting for your wife to show up.'

'He's right,' Pani said solemnly. 'Sedna got in a fight with the wolf too, and the rest of the dogs were very scared.'

Tom Ellison nodded. 'Ben and Gaborik are bedding them down in an old storehouse near the pit entrance.'

'Show us,' said Simonie. Concern for his dogs was clear in his face.

'We'll stay here and look after Nanook,' Pani offered.

Simonie nodded gratefully, then sighed. 'I wish I knew why Nanook risked her life to protect a wolf. She's always been a loner but

she's never attacked one of the dogs before
. . .' He opened the cabin door. 'Ready,
Adam?'

Mr Hope nodded, and the three men went
outside. The heavy door shut out the worst
of the Arctic chill behind them.

'I was right when I said this would be a
trip to remember!' Mandy sighed, slumping
back down on to the box of food. 'And it's
not over yet!'

'Let's open a tin,' Pani suggested, crossing
to Nanook and gently stroking her head. 'I'm
starving!'

'I suppose Thomas Tupilak won't be
needing them any more,' Mandy agreed.
Soon she had joined her friend at the table
with a tin of baked beans and a can opener.

Just then, Nanook's eyes flickered open.
She licked her lips with a dry tongue, and
Mandy pushed the plate of water nearer the
dog's mouth. This time, Nanook drank
properly.

'Good girl, Nanook,' Pani whispered, her eyes shining with joy.

Mandy smiled as she fetched two plates and opened the tin of beans. The day seemed to have lasted for ever. Now, with her dad here, Thomas Tupilak gone and her mum on the way, maybe things would be all right.

Eleven

When Mandy woke up and blearily rubbed her eyes, it took her a few moments to work out where she was. The first rays of the wintry sun were shining into the back of the Nanogaks' truck as it trundled along the winding roads back to Kimmirut.

Pani was still fast asleep, her head resting against Mandy's shoulder. Curled up in a blanket next to them was Nanook. Her breathing was deep and even, and Mandy smiled to herself with relief.

Emily Hope had arrived in the truck with Mary in the middle of the night. Between sneezes and shivers, she'd bathed Nanook's cut with antiseptic and put in some stitches. She agreed with Mandy's dad that the brave husky would definitely be OK.

Simonie and Gaborik had sorted out everything else. Gaborik had taken Tom Ellison and Ben Page back to the camping lodge with Simonie's husky team before returning to the hut for the night. Mary dropped Simonie off at the lodge on the way back, so he could check on both his dogs and the patient tourists. Gaborik would journey by sled over to the lodge in the morning and, together, he and Simonie would take everyone back to Kimmirut.

Mary had driven the rest of them back home through the night. Mandy stretched back on the warm, cracked-leather seat and yawned happily. After all their freezing adventures it was blissful to feel so snug and warm.

An hour or so later the truck slowed bumpily to a halt.

Pani woke up and blinked. 'We're home!'

'Comfy bed, here I come,' Emily Hope muttered from the front of the truck.

Adam Hope got out and opened the door beside Nanook. 'Come on then,' he said to the dog. 'Let's get you back to your kennel.'

Nanook stirred a little and then whimpered as Adam and Emily Hope eased her back on to her stretcher.

'Mandy and I can take her, Mr Hope,' said Pani.

'All right, you two,' Emily Hope agreed. 'But be very gentle.'

Mandy nodded. Carefully, the two girls carried Nanook down to the dog yard. As they reached the gate, a sound rang out that Mandy recognised with a thrill of fear. It was the sound of a wolf howling.

'Wolves don't normally venture this close to town,' Pani said, puzzled.

Nanook's eyes widened and her ears pricked up at the sound of the wolf's lonely cry. She struggled to get up.

'It's all right, girl,' Mandy said gently. 'Don't be scared. The wolf's far away, it's not going to hurt you.'

But Pani shook her head thoughtfully, and gently scratched the coarse fur behind Nanook's ears. She was looking more serious than Mandy had ever seen her.

'I know my dogs,' she said quietly, 'especially Nanook. That isn't fear in her eyes, I'm sure of it. It's something else.'

Mandy spent most of the day asleep. When she woke, the sun was starting to set and she could hear the sound of excited voices and laughter in the room below. Dressing quickly, she ran downstairs to see what was happening.

She found everyone in the kitchen. Gaborik was pouring a mug of tea for himself and for Simonie. Mary and Pani stood beside her dad. Even her mum was up and about.

'What's going on?' Mandy asked.

'Hi, Mandy! Come and join the celebrations!' Pani grinned.

'What celebrations?' she said, puzzled.

Gaborik grinned. 'No more Thomas Tupilak to worry about!'

'The police picked him up at Iqaluit Airport, trying to leave the island,' Simonie explained. 'After I showed them the files this morning, and Mr Ellison explained what services Tupilak was offering, they decided they had some serious questions to put to him.'

'But what about his dogs? Who'll look after them?' Mandy burst out.

'Dad's going to buy them!' Pani said excitedly.

'It's just an idea,' Simonie explained. 'But if Tupilak can no longer offer sled tours in the area, perhaps I should think about expanding my business.'

'I think it's a great idea,' said Adam Hope, raising a glass of water in a toast. 'Cheers, Simonie. Here's to a bright future.'

Everyone raised a glass, except Mandy who helped herself to her dad's. She drained it dry and licked her lips. 'Thanks, Dad!' she grinned. 'So how's Nanook?'

'Resting with the others,' said Mary Nanogak. 'They've all been through a lot. They've earned some time off!'

'Nanook seems better already,' Gaborik told her. 'She was able to stand up this morning.'

'Don't let her walk too far,' warned Emily Hope. 'That leg is badly sprained, she must rest it as much as possible.'

'She'll probably try to bite at the bandage round her neck too,' Mr Hope added. 'Keep an eye on her. You can always get a special plastic collar to fit over her head to stop her if necessary.'

Mary nodded. 'Thank you for all you've done for her.'

'Lucky for us we have on-site medical help!' Simonie agreed.

Everyone laughed and cheered. Then Pani noticed the clock on the wall. 'It's almost five o'clock. The party in the *akavak* centre will be starting soon!'

'*Akavak?*' echoed Mandy blankly.

'Our community centre,' Pani explained, bubbling with excitement. 'Every Wednesday there's a big festival. Music and dancing and craft and sports and . . . *everything*!'

'Sounds great!' Mandy grinned.

'Grandad will be there too,' Pani went on. 'We can ask him about Nanook and the wolf.'

Mandy remembered the way Nanook had reacted when the wolf had howled that morning. She hoped that Solomon would be able to solve the mystery. 'Let's go and look at Nanook before we go,' she suggested.

Pani led the way out to the yard. Okpik ran out to greet them both, barking noisily. He scampered about them as they headed for Nanook's kennel. The gate to her run had been left open, so she could walk around the exercise yard if she wanted to.

Mandy peered inside the warm kennel. 'She's standing up!' she said with delight. Nanook looked up at them both, her eyes bright and alert, her tail slowly wagging.

'She's getting stronger all the time,' said Pani proudly. 'By the time we get back from the party I bet she'll be racing round the yard!'

The community centre was built on the beachfront, and it wasn't long before the Nanogaks' truck was pulling up in the small, gravelled car park. Mandy and Pani ran on ahead of their parents, and soon they reached the narrow path that led down to the beach. Under the dark sky, the ocean hissed over the icy shore like a vast shifting shadow.

'I'm used to seeing sand on the beach, not snow,' Mandy said.

'Sand? Weird!' Pani laughed.

As they approached the centre, the sound of rhythmic drumming could be heard. Wooden posts holding flaming torches had been erected outside the building's entrance. The flickering fires licked at the dark sky as if dancing to the beat.

Once inside, Mandy decided it was a bit like a massive indoor fête. There were people everywhere, bustling about, crowding in huddles talking or else sitting with snacks at tables. There were displays of crafts, and stalls had been set up with all kinds of goods. The people of Kimmirut greeted Pani in Inuktitut and smiled at Mandy in welcome.

'See what I mean?' said Pani. 'There's everything here!'

'And every*one*, too, by the looks of things!' Mandy replied. A woman in a black coat with a bright red scarf squeezed past her. She looked familiar.

'Mrs Ellison!' Mandy cried, and the woman turned in surprise.

'Hello Mandy!' she said with a wide smile. 'And Pani. How are you two doing?'

'We're great, thank you,' Pani told her. 'Especially since your husband and Mr Page helped the police catch Thomas Tupilak!'

Mrs Ellison shuddered. 'It was the least they could've done after all the trouble they'd caused.' Then she smiled. 'Still, that's all over now.'

'Where are they?' Mandy asked.

'Over there.' Mrs Ellison pointed over to a stall in the corner, where Mr Ellison and Ben Page seemed to be haggling with the owner. 'The only thing those two are going to be hunting for around here are some presents for me! After stranding me in the middle of nowhere they've got a lot of making up to do!'

Mandy and Pani both laughed, and Mrs Ellison winked and waved goodbye.

The two of them pushed on through the noisy crowd. Mandy was amazed by the array of things to see. One stall was selling colourful hand-sewn socks and knitted hats called *tuques*. In a room just off the main hall, a group of women were performing an intricate dance to the pounding rhythm of the native drums. Mandy happily tapped along with her foot.

'Grandad!' Pani yelled over the noise.

Mandy turned to see the kindly face of Solomon moving through the crowd towards them. Behind him came Simonie, Mary, Gaborik and Mr and Mrs Hope. Pani rushed up to the old man and gave him a hug.

'Simonie says you two have things you

wish to ask me,' he said. He frowned as the noise of the drums grew louder as the Inuit dance neared its end. 'Perhaps we should talk outside?'

Mandy and Pani followed him out on to the frozen beach, both eagerly describing Nanook's strange behaviour.

Solomon's eyes narrowed as he listened. Then he stopped and nodded his head. 'You know, I am an old man now,' he began in his slow, careful English. 'But I can still remember . . . Many years ago, when I left the old mine, I bought my first Canadian Inuit dog from the owner. This dog was one of Nanook's grandmothers. Her name was Alainga.'

Mandy and Pani listened intently, entranced by the unfolding story.

'When Nanook was born four generations later, she looked exactly like Alainga. The same build, the same colouring . . . even the fold on her ear was the same.' Solomon smiled at the memory. 'She was a good girl,

Alainga. Strong and loyal and brave. And she had a fierce streak in her too. I suspected then that one of *her* grandsires was a wolf.'

Pani's eyes opened very wide. 'A wolf?'

Solomon nodded and patted her shoulder. 'The ties between family are strong. They do not grow weak with the years.' He smiled again. 'Perhaps this is why Nanook acted as she did.'

'No wonder you called her a lone wolf,' Mandy breathed. 'When Sedna attacked the wolf in the gully, maybe Nanook felt she was attacking a part of *her*.'

Solomon didn't say anything, but he nodded his head.

'Thank you, Grandad,' said Pani, giving him a hug.

Solomon shrugged. 'I have only told you the thoughts of an old man.' He shivered. 'An old man who is ready to rejoin the party! Shall we go?' Jauntily linking arms with them, he led them back inside.

* * *

It was quite late when Mandy and her family headed home with the Nanogaks. Waving goodbye to Gaborik, they set off once more in the truck.

'I feel like I've been here for ages and ages,' said Mandy, staring dreamily out of the window. 'I can't believe we'll be going back home on Saturday.'

'This whole trip has been incredible,' Mr Hope agreed. 'Seals, polar bears, huskies and caribou . . . Still, there's Animal Ark waiting for us when we get back. And Gran and Grandad.'

'And James and Blackie,' Mrs Hope chimed in.

'And *everyone* in Welford,' Mandy agreed. The thought of all the things she knew so well had sparked off a pang of homesickness. 'It'll be great to see everyone again. I just hope that maybe we can come back some day.'

'Me too,' said Pani with a shy smile.

Leaving the truck, Mandy and Pani led the way up the driveway to the Nanogaks' home. The house was silent, and dark save for the frost on the woodwork, sparkling in the light of the moon.

'Let's check Nanook's not running about without her bandage,' said Pani, and the two of them walked on to the dog yard. Suddenly Pani froze. She grabbed Mandy's arm and pointed. 'Look!' she whispered. 'There, by the trees!'

Mandy peered into the gloom. At first, all she could see were trees and snow. Then she gasped, as a wolf came out of the whiteness beneath the conifers and into the open.

As it drew nearer, Mandy recognised the distinctive grey smudges on the animal's side. 'I'm sure it's the one we saw in the gully! It's come so far. . .' she whispered in amazement.

'And look,' said Pani, clutching at Mandy's

coat sleeve excitedly. 'There's Nanook!'

Limping out of her kennel, her black nose twitching, Nanook padded across the yard towards the wolf.

Mandy knew she was witnessing something truly special as dog and wolf stood face to face, just metres away from her. The wolf looked at Nanook, the yellow of its eyes catching the moonlight. Nanook stared back. Neither animal made a sound, but their plumy tails wagged slowly in unison.

After a long minute, the wolf turned and trotted back over to the tree line. It stopped, looked back, and gave a low, mournful howl.

'It's saying thank you,' Mandy whispered, shaking her head in wonder. 'Thank you and goodbye.'

Nanook barked twice in return. Then the wolf turned away and vanished back into the night.